BREAKING POINT

ALSO BY BRADLEY WRIGHT

Alexander King

THE SECRET WEAPON

COLD WAR

MOST WANTED

POWER MOVE

ENEMY LINES

SMOKE SCREEN

SPY RING

WAR MACHINE

Alexander King Prequels

WHISKEY & ROSES

VANQUISH

KING'S RANSOM

KING'S REIGN

SCOURGE

Tom Walker

Killer Instinct

Holy Water

Blind Pass

Deliverance

Lawson Raines

WHEN THE MAN COMES AROUND

SHOOTING STAR

Saint Nick

SAINT NICK

SAINT NICK 2

ALSO BY J.D. DUDYCHA

First Coast Adventure Series

Coastal Pursuit

Seaside Heist

Gage Finley Adventures

Scavengers

Dark Descent

Buried Secrets

Deep Blue

Hurricane

Niki Finley Thrillers

First Shot

Second Best

Third Degree

BREAKING POINT

Bradley Wright/King's Ransom Publishing
www.bradleywrightauthor.com
Publisher's Note: This is a work of fiction. Names, characters, places, and incidents are a product of the author's imagination. Locales and public names are sometimes used for atmospheric purposes. Any resemblance to actual people, living or dead, or to businesses, companies, events, institutions, or locales is completely coincidental.
BREAKING POINT/Bradley Wright. 1st ed. ISBN - 9798345195598

This one is for our parents. Always having someone in your corner might be the most underrated thing in the human experience. Thanks for everything. We love you.

The world is full of monsters with friendly faces and angels with scars.

— HEATHER BREWER

BREAKING POINT

PROLOGUE

A DEAD MAN FLOATED FACE DOWN IN A PRISTINE RECTANGULAR pool. Saam Rajabi stood on the ornate tile of the pool deck and stared at the man he had just shot. He surveyed the water surrounding his victim as it turned a deep shade of red. Bored of watching blood cloud his pool, Rajabi changed his perspective and studied the palm trees that surrounded the perimeter of his home. Home may have been an understatement—residential castle was a better word. An eight-thousand-square-foot fortress carved out of imported marble and stone.

Gunshots rang out in the distance. Rajabi didn't flinch at their sound. It was as if he expected those shots to come. And why wouldn't they? Outside his walls was unrest. A civil war that had spanned many years. But that instability never made it to his doorstep because of his reputation. He was the one fueling the lies through media outlets, politicians, businessmen, rebel forces, terror groups—anyone he could bribe to further his own agenda. Which gave him many allies, and everyone knew it best not to bring the fight to him.

"Sir." A man showed up from behind Rajabi and paid no attention to the dead man floating in the pool.

"What is it, Cyrus?"

Cyrus stood about six feet tall and weighed about 230 pounds. Not overly fat—he was thick. Muscular.

"There's a phone call for you. It's Dimitri. He needs your attention. And you're going to want to hear what he has to say."

Rajabi nodded toward the dead man in the water. "Take care of the trash defiling my pool."

"Yes, sir."

Rajabi stepped through an archway that connected his veranda and a courtyard. The courtyard was open to the elements, which allowed overgrown vines to crawl up the pillars toward the second-level windows. They weren't unsightly; in fact, they added to the character of the design.

An octagon-shaped fountain was erected in the center of the courtyard. Rajabi loved sitting there. He would stare inside the water feature, listening as the stream splashed like a light rain. The sound soothed him. Always had, but he couldn't stop and sit for a listen now. Cyrus wasn't the type of man to interrupt Rajabi often. If Cyrus said Rajabi needed to take the call, it was likely the news couldn't wait.

Once inside, Rajabi moved toward a television and sat on the oversize red couch beneath it. The broadcast playing on the screen was an American news outlet. He needed it on because of his interest in two specific Americans he had been tracking. Turned out to be a dead end because of the tight lips of the dead man in his pool. Rajabi reached for the telephone on the end table and lifted the receiver.

"Dimitri," Rajabi said.

"I found the Americans," Dimitri said with a thick Russian accent.

"Good. Where?"

"They fled Damascus just before the missile strike went off in the northern part of the city. I assume they had intel that the strike was coming. Maybe even called it in. My men tracked them as far as the southern border, but then lost them in the mountains before they could cut them off."

"They cannot cross over into Israel, Dimitri. Not even into Golan Heights. ISIS controls that area. And if they get their hands on them, they'll kill them instantly. You know how important the Americans are. What they have in their possession. If another terrorist cell or the

Israeli army gets their hands on it . . . or even the American government . . ." Rajabi trailed off.

"My men will track them down and trap them before that happens."

"Trap them? How?"

Before Dimitri could come back with an answer, the line went dead.

Rajabi took the phone from his ear and stared at the receiver. "Dimitri. Dimitri."

He slammed the phone down, then grabbed the remote for the TV and chucked it hard against his wall. Cyrus returned just as the remote exploded and the batteries went flying.

Cyrus waited for Rajabi to speak, which was customary for him. He rarely spoke out of turn.

Rajabi sat for a moment, deep in thought, watching the images of the fights in Gaza play on a loop. The American news outlet continued their slanted viewpoint about how bad the fighting was and what it would take to put an end to the war—as if they had any idea.

But Rajabi knew better. The war would never end. Not until every unbeliever was killed. That was how far he was willing to go.

"Ready the car," Rajabi told Cyrus. "I'm not waiting for Dimitri. We're going after the Americans. Even if I have to track them all the way back to Washington myself, I will find them. And I will kill them."

CHAPTER ONE

"WELCOME TO HELL, EMILY," ADAM BURKE SAID, CHUCKLING. "Hell's Revenge that is."

Burke stood atop a rock formation and stared down along the jagged sandstone ridge where he was preparing to drive his four-by-four. Hell's Revenge, a fitting name, was one of the most iconic off-road trails in the entire world.

"I don't know about this, Burke," Emily Kilpatrick said, holding her hands on her hips.

"What's not to know? You asked for training."

"Yeah, training in combat. Not bouldering down a mountain, riding inside a truck with no top or doors."

"Relax. We got roll bars if anything crazy happens. Besides, it's not like you can come to Moab and not experience this. We didn't come out to Jonesy's house for the milk and cookies. You asked for training. And over the last few weeks you've done well with weapons and hand-to-hand, and limited pool training, but that was basic. Now, well, this—let's consider this the beginning of your special warfare training. Now get in."

Burke walked to the driver's side and stepped through the vacant opening. He pushed in the clutch and turned the key. The truck fired up right away, but Emily waited in the same spot Burke had left her—still staring at the trail ahead of them. She shook her head, and Burke couldn't tell what she had muttered to herself.

"*Hey*," he yelled out the top of the roofless vehicle and over the windshield. "Let's go. Get in."

Emily turned around and shook her head, still mumbling to herself. Once inside, she looked over at Burke, who was smiling at her insecurity. Before she uttered another word, Burke rammed the stick shift into first gear, let out the clutch, and slammed his foot down on the gas pedal. Emily yelped and covered her head with her hands as they descended the trail.

The rock formations seemed to extend for miles. Even stretching as far as the horizon line. And there were trees scattered throughout the rocks, growing inside the small crevices at the base of each rolling hogback.

Once they reached the foundation of the first rock formation, there was a long straightaway up to another ridge. Burke downshifted and revved his RPMs as he sped up the bumpy path. Emily let out a yelp as she held on to the roll bar above her head while her body rocked from side to side.

She stared at him and said in a shaky voice, "You're enjoying this, aren't you?"

He gleamed. "With every fiber of my being."

Once over the cusp, the trail snaked downward, and for a brief second the ground seemed to disappear from existence.

"Uh, Burke." Emily stretched across and grabbed onto his right shoulder. "Wait . . . wait." She sucked in short breaths.

"Calm yourself down, Emily. We're fine. Just breathe."

Burke proceeded. He looked to his left and out the empty doorway to see the rock formations descend into an extreme drop-off. With every rise and fall of the motion of the truck, Emily went rigid.

"This is way worse than you said it was gonna be," she said.

Burke stopped driving, and the vehicle was leaning forward and to the side, like at any moment it could tumble over and carry them over the rock's edge. "But it *is* necessary."

She shot him a look, then turned to look out the open door to her right. "Necessary for what?"

"To see how you react. To see if you're comfortable in uncomfortable situations. That's what this is, Emily. That's what combat will be like. I knew you'd be afraid of this. We need to know . . . that we can trust you in crazy situations. That I can trust you with my life—with Jonesy's—Mack's. All of ours."

"So that's what this is?" Emily looked around the topography. "Your idea of some kind of test?"

"Yep." He nodded. "See, when you're in special operations training, it's not the strongest physically who move on. It's the strongest mentally." Burke pointed to his head. "And since you lack the physical size of most enemies you'll encounter, you have to rely on your brain and your resolve to get you through."

Burke spun the wheel to his left and continued driving down the trail, and he didn't stop again until they reached their biggest challenge yet.

"What's this? Why are we stopping? And why are there a line of cars waiting?" Emily said.

"Because the Hell's Revenge trail was just the beginning." Burke rolled his head and signified what they had just done. "This next part is called Hell's Gate. We just drove down the first part of Hell's Gate, but now it's a near-vertical climb up a wall of rock. And our only way out."

"Wonderful." She threw her hands up in the air.

Emily stepped outside the door after Burke put the vehicle in park. There were five cars ahead of them waiting to make the climb. Burke and Emily walked forward until they could see another vehicle bouldering up the rock. Burke wanted her to see what to expect.

"That's steep, Burke." She stared at him. He didn't respond. Then she spoke again with more urgency. "Like really steep."

Again the sides of his mouth turned up. Then they turned to walk back to their vehicle. It didn't take long for them to move forward in line, and once the fifth car made its approach, Burke pulled forward.

"We're on deck. Any last thoughts, maybe send up a prayer to the Big Guy," Burke said.

"Very funny, Burke."

"I'm not joking. People have died on this rock, Emily. If you want to get anything off your chest with me or, you know, God, now's your chance."

Burke played on her emotions. He wasn't entirely serious, nor did he have any idea if anyone had died on that rock, but ultimately, he wanted to plant a seed of fear.

She shook her head and ground her teeth. "I hate you for this," she said.

"Oh, come on. There's nothing to worry about. I got this."

"Famous last words of every man about to fall from grace," she said.

When they came to the base of the rock, Emily leaned forward to look skyward. From where they were, the sun cast a shadow over the rock about halfway into their path. Emily made a move to shield her eyes with her hand so she could see.

"That's a long way up, Burke."

"Sure is."

"You sure it's safe?"

"Don't know. Never done it before."

"Wait, *what*?" Emily shouted. "I thought you said you can't come to Moab without experiencing this."

"That's true."

"So, uh, I'm confused."

"About what?"

"Have you never experienced this before?"

"Sure."

"I still don't get it."

"This is my first time driving the trail. Usually I ride up here with Jonesy."

"So why didn't he bring me here instead of you?"

"Because I wanted to see if I could handle being comfortable in uncomfortable situations." He grinned. "Training never ends, Emily. Not even for me."

She sighed, then stared up at the cloudless pale blue sky.

Burke took her silence for the perfect opportunity to ascend. He took it slowly. The climb wasn't easy, and the path a driver has to take up Hell's Gate is difficult to navigate. But it was one Burke had the confidence to conquer.

Once his rugged knobby tires met the hard rock, the truck lifted. And at that moment, Emily reached across and grabbed hold of Burke again. He didn't even scold her or notice how tight she was holding his arm; he was too focused on his task at hand. The truck ascended at a forty-five-degree angle, and soon it would turn even more vertical as they continued. Halfway up, Burke could feel the trail becoming more difficult to traverse.

He heard the spotter from the top of the trail yelling downward, "*Passenger*," signifying he needed to turn the vehicle to his right. He did as he was instructed but spun too far to his right, and his knobby tire fell into a crack. He needed to reverse out of the crack.

"Oh my gosh, oh my gosh. What are you doing? What are you doing?" Emily gripped Burke's arm and went flat against her seat.

Burke turned over his shoulder and backed up out of the hole to give the climb another try. Once he got back on track, he drove upward. At that point the truck was at a near seventy-degree angle. Emily pinched Burke's shoulder with her tight grip, but he couldn't respond. He just needed to press on. Slowly but surely, he could not stop the momentum of the climb.

As he inched forward, his back right tire got pinched between the rock and the wheel.

"*Passenger*. *Passenger*!" the scout yelled from above.

But it was too late. The tire popped, which made the truck lurch forward. And with the steep angle, the hood started rising until it was standing almost straight up in the air, the vehicle lying on its tailgate, only inches from tipping over backward and tumbling back down the path they had just ascended.

CHAPTER TWO

Burke's arms went stiff on the steering wheel, and he felt the powerful rays of the sun warm his thick hair through the vacant roof hole. He took a quick glance at Emily. She was ghost white as all the blood rushed from her face and she stared through the windshield and up toward the sky but refused to say anything.

"Get the winch." Burke heard the spotter say from ahead. "*Now*! H*urry*, before it goes over!"

Burke's heart was in his throat. He stayed still because any sudden movement could send them tumbling end over end.

"Hear that? Everything's gonna be fine." Burke refused to let his fear be known.

"*Fine?*" She shot him a look. "This is your idea of *fine?*"

"Hey, before the trip up here, I did promise you an adventure of a lifetime."

She scowled at him, just as the spotter approached Burke's door.

"Sir, we've got you," the spotter said. They couldn't see him, but Burke knew he was close. "We're getting a winch now. Once we get the steel rope wrapped around your bumper, we'll pull you back onto four wheels. So just sit tight."

Easy for him to say. "*Sit tight*" in a four-thousand-pound truck that could roll over at any moment onto an unforgiving rock and cause who knows what kind of damage. Not that Burke cared about the truck; it was his life and Emily's that were far more valuable.

"So . . . are you?" Burke said.

"Am I what? Pissed at you?" Emily said. "I think that goes without saying."

"No. Comfortable." Burke grinned. "I mean, I never thought I'd be locked in this precarious position. It's almost like we're about to be shot up into space like a rocket."

"Of course," Emily said, shaking her head. "Only you could make light of all this."

"What am I supposed to do? Be mad? Sad? Scared? No way. I may have to change my boxers after this one, but hey, it just adds to the excitement of the climb. Who else has this story? I guarantee not one other vehicle has been lodged on Hell's Gate like this. No chance. I think maybe the big guy upstairs was looking out for us on this one."

"Sure, Burke, maybe. But still. This is not my idea of fun. Next time, just let Jonesy do the driving."

The spotter cut in. "All right, sir, we've got the rope. I'll be attaching it now."

Burke's eyes danced around the dashboard. Both he and Emily heard jangling from beneath the vehicle. He wanted to know what was happening; not being able to see made him feel helpless. And for a guy like Burke, helplessness was not a feeling he enjoyed.

"Got it tethered," the spotter told Burke and then yelled back up the mountain, "*Hit it*!"

The truck leaned forward, but only just a little. Emily let out a yelp and Burke chuckled. When the truck's energy carried it backward after the forward lurch, Burke's smile faded.

"Oh, sh—" Before Burke finished his thought, the winch rope came tight and yanked the truck forward. The truck crashed down and bounced off the rock once the front tires made contact. "*Woo hoo*," Burke shouted. "That was awesome." He found Emily's eyes again. She did not share his enthusiasm.

She lowered her head, annoyed, and glared at him just as the spotter came into view over the hood of the truck.

"Y'all good in there?"

Burke checked on Emily.

"Yep. Never better." Burke gave him two thumbs up.

"You both sure had a wild ride. And now you have one incredible story to tell."

"See." Burke tapped Emily on the shoulder. "Even he thinks that was cool."

"You're an idiot, Burke."

"That may be true, but . . ."

"But what?"

"At least I'm an idiot with a story."

The spotter walked closer to the truck and leaned into Burke's window. "Y'all got a spare tire in here?"

Burke nodded and tipped his head. "Sure do. In the back."

"Good. We'll winch you up the rest of the way. Just take it slow. When you reach the top, let's change your tire and get you out of here."

"Sounds like a plan," Burke said.

Burke steered up the rock. The winch was doing most of the work. As they climbed, Burke did exactly what the spotter had told him to do. When he came to the top, the crowd of at least thirty people cheered their arrival. Burke pumped his fists to appease the mob. Emily gave him a sour look.

"What? I can't disappoint my people."

"You're unbelievable."

"Thank you. I take that as a compliment coming from you."

The spotter came close and said, "Hop out and let's get that tire changed. Then we can get you going so you can try to drop into the *Hot Tub*."

Burke and the spotter shared a laugh, knowing what the *Hot Tub* entailed—a bowl-like formation carved inside the rock.

"Hot Tub?" Emily said. "Out here on the rocks?"

"Not like the ones you might be used to, doll." The spotter winked.

"Oh, no." Emily reached for the door to step out of the truck. "I'm not doing this anymore."

"Okay, fine," Burke said. "We'll skip the Hot Tub." He stepped outside and shook the spotter's hand. "Thanks for all your help."

A shrill whistle came from behind, and someone from the crowd yelled out, "Uh, Dickie. Hey man, we're gonna need you over here again."

The spotter stepped away from Burke and Emily and said, "Sorry, guys, gotta go. Duty calls."

Burke looked over at Emily and said, "Ever change a tire before?"

"Of course. What do you think I am, some kind of helpless princess?"

"Hey, never know these days. Especially with the way most kids are raised."

"You forget I was raised by a Marine."

"No. Never. I love hearing stories about your father. The man was a legend."

"Yeah, he was."

"Let's see how well he taught you then, shall we?"

Burke reached for the tailgate and ripped it open to grab the spare tire out of the bed of the truck. As Burke pulled out the tire, he lost sight of what Emily was doing. For the first time since they had arrived on the trail, she grabbed her cell phone and perused.

When he noticed her on her phone, he said, "Can't get away from that thing for one second, can you?"

She didn't respond. He saw a perplexed look lingering on her face, like she was reading something shocking. "What is it?"

She showed him the phone. It was a breaking news story: "*Two American Journalists Reported Missing. Last Known Whereabouts Damascus, Syria.*"

Burke scrunched his brow. "That sucks." Burke sensed that his flippant response didn't match Emily's concern.

Emily kept reading the story. "I know her."

Burke looked on. "Who?"

"One of the missing reporters."

"What? You do? Were their names released to the public?" He circled around her to look for himself.

"Not yet. But I just know."

"How?"

"She's a friend. We played soccer at Duke together. Both of us went to work in Roanoke for a newspaper. But when I went on to work for the CIA, she continued pursuing the reporter angle. Always wanted to be in the action. Ended up with the *New York Times* for a bit. She wanted to be sent to the Middle East, Africa, wherever, to break stories from the front lines of war. Remember that story I told about those American tourists who were beheaded in Lebanon?"

Burke nodded; he remembered the story well.

"She was there with me. I used her camera to take the photos."

"You're kidding me?"

"I'm not."

"So, how do you know she's there now?" Burke stared off at the approaching vehicle who had just finished the climb.

Emily brought the phone close to her face and thumbed her way to her text messages. "Because this morning she sent me this. Got the text just as we arrived up here." She showed him her phone again, and immediately Burke's eyes grew wide as he read.

The photo featured a man and a woman at ground zero in the middle of a war zone, with the message, "Damascus."

"Why did she send you this photo?" Burke said.

"No idea, Burke. Didn't think much of it at the time. I haven't spoken to her in years. Maybe three or four."

Emily flipped the phone back around.

"What is it?"

"Just got another text."

Emily's face went whiter than when she was stuck in the truck at a ninety-degree angle.

"What?" Burke said.

She showed Burke her phone again. There was only one word written.

Help!

CHAPTER THREE

BURKE DROVE DOWN A SINGLE-LANE DIRT ROAD THAT LED TO JONES'S property. The property itself was over six acres and carved out of red rock and cottonwood trees. A rushing stream cut the property in half and was fed from the frozen runoff of the La Sal Mountains. Burke drove over the land bridge that the brook ducked under, and he looked to his left to watch the water rush over the edge and cascade into the waiting deep pool below.

"I never get sick of this view," Burke said as he looked through the hole of the doorless truck.

Emily kept quiet, not that she didn't hear Burke; rather, she was still trying to get more of the story on her missing friend from the news articles she perused on her phone.

Burke stopped in front of Jones's meager residence. The house wasn't dilapidated; Jones was simply prouder of the property than the house itself.

Jones stood on the crushed-rock driveway unloading his Jeep Wrangler when Burke parked. Burke watched him step away from his Jeep and study the truck Burke was driving.

"He knows something's up," Burke said.

"'Course he does. He's not some dumb schmuck. You wrecked his truck."

"Did not." Burke snapped back.

"Did too. At the very least, damaged his tailgate beyond repair."

"It could've been a lot worse."

Jones stepped wide and eyed the driver's side. "Looks like you didn't beat her up too badly." He sounded surprised.

"What?" Burke rubbed the back of his head. "Uh, yeah, yeah. You're right, not too bad."

Emily shot through the vacant roof and yelled, "Wait until you see the tailgate."

"*Emily*." Burke reached for her, threatening to pull her down playfully.

She swatted his hand away and continued. "We almost went end over end."

Jones looked confused as he continued toward the rear of the truck.

Burke jumped out through the door frame and cut his friend off. "Where you goin'?"

"Apparently I'm going to assess the damage on the back of my truck."

"Not necessary. We got it all figured out. Even got you a new tire." Burke kicked it on the way by.

"What happened to the old one?" Jones said.

Burke held his tongue. He didn't know how mad his friend would be knowing he almost flipped the truck over.

"Think it was just time, ya know. Tires don't last forever."

"But they *do* last more than six months. I just got these."

They finally worked their way around toward the back end. Once Jones was looking over the rear, Burke smirked. "Well, at least they should still be under warranty then."

Jones shot Burke a look. "Ya think?" Jones reached for the rear and rubbed his hand over the damage. "So what happened? At least tell me there was a cool story behind the accident."

"See." Burke found Emily's eyes. "Even Jonesy appreciates a good story behind the scars."

Emily tilted her head.

"Tire popped going up Hell's Gate. Once that happened, I let the clutch out too soon, and the truck lurched forward. Ended up standing on its back end. Like we were about to be shot into space like a missile."

"Really?" Jones was almost impressed. He curled his lower lip. "Nice."

"What? Seriously?" Emily couldn't believe their banter. "That's all you have to say? *Nice*? We could've been killed. And your truck, it's . . . it's ruined."

Jones turned his attention to the rear end. "Nah. This is nothing. This truck's seen a lot worse. Trust me. That's what it's for anyway. Banging away on Hell's Revenge."

"I can't believe you two idiots. Remind me never to accept another free trip to Moab." Emily began to walk away.

Burke and Jones shared a smile. Just as Emily walked away, Jones said to both of them, "By the way, Stallone called. Wants to have a chat with us about our next mission."

"Mission?" Burke said. "Really?"

"Apparently, he's got some intel on some missing journalists in the Middle East."

Emily whipped around. "What—are you serious?"

Confusion lingered on Jones's face. "Uh, I think so. Said to contact him right away. Even said you'd be especially interested in the mission. Something about an old friend of yours, I think." Jones wasn't sure he remembered correctly. Emily's eyes found the ground. Jones could tell something was off. "What is it?"

She didn't respond, but Burke did. "She got a text while we were up the mountain."

"A text?"

"Yeah. From the girl. One of the missing journalists."

"Wait, one of the missing journalists is the friend Stallone was talking about?" Jones finally caught up.

Burke nodded.

Emily raised her head and said, "What are we waiting for? Let's go call Stallone."

Emily walked ahead of Burke and Jones almost in a light jog. The men witnessed her expedience, so they followed suit with a quickened pace.

"Dang, Burke, I had no idea," Jones said as they jogged.

"Me either, Jonesy. She didn't really know anything either. Not until we got on the top of Hell's Gate. Had no idea why she reached out in the first place. Emily said it had been years since they last spoke."

"What'd the girl say in the text?"

"She sent a picture labeled Damascus. Then another with only one word. Help."

"Help? How did she know that Emily could help her?"

Burke shrugged just as they entered Jones's living room. There was a TV hanging on the wall. Jones flipped it on, and a few seconds later, Avery Stallone appeared on the sixty-five-inch screen.

"Good, you're all there," Stallone said.

All three stared at him. He was in a conference room set up with over a dozen chairs, but only one other person occupied a chair in that room. Lily Ann Wallenby. A tech expert—a surprisingly young tech expert, but one of the best in the agency.

"Where's Danny?" Burke asked. Danny had been with them on their previous mission.

"Danny's been reassigned."

"Couldn't hack it, huh? Pun intended." Burke spoke the next words out of the side of his mouth so only Jones and Emily could hear. "Guy was a liability."

"What was that?" Stallone replied.

"Nothing, sir. Just getting Jones up to speed with the team."

"Good. Then I'll let Lily catch you up with what we know."

"Burke! Oh, thank God. It is *so* good to see you again, even if it is through a TV screen," Lily said, grinning from ear to ear.

Burke smiled at Jones who couldn't help but snicker at her overzealous response.

"Lily—that's enough." Stallone reprimanded her. "Get on with it."

"Right. Sorry."

Lily looked down at her tablet and swiped along, causing her screen to appear on Jones's TV. Pictures of the two missing journalists. Burke looked at Emily. Her concern was undeniable, but she nodded to let Burke know one of the journalists was her friend.

"The woman pictured is Veronica Alberts. Goes by the nickname V," Lily said.

Again, Emily nodded in agreement.

"The man with her is named Gilberto Lopez. Their last known whereabouts were somewhere outside Damascus, Syria. Apparently, they were close to the missile strike in the northern part of the city but made it out alive."

"Do we have any intelligence that suggests what they were doing in Damascus?" Jones said.

"Yes. They are in possession of a flash drive. Stolen from a terror group with ties to Lebanon, Palestine, Iran, Syria, just to name a few," Stallone said.

"That's more than a few." Burke nudged Jones.

Then Emily cut in. "Wait, what? What are they doing with a stolen flash drive. V's not CIA . . ." Emily trailed off. "She was just there trying to get a story from the front lines, right? From the Hamas–Israeli conflict?"

Stallone stood stoic. Silent at first. "Are you certain she's not CIA?"

Emily's mouth hung open. She leaned forward and waited for his response with bated breath.

"You think you were the only journalist Naomi recruited during her time—the only asset she used throughout her career?"

"That's impossible. V would've told me."

"She would've been a horrible operative if she had divulged too much by telling you," Stallone said.

Emily continued to mumble to herself in disbelief.

"So what's the mission?" Burke piped up.

"Find them. Extract both V and Lopez and obtain the flash drive. It's vital to your mission and to national security."

"National security? How?" Burke said.

Stallone spoke up, a little louder than before. "For one—because intelligence dictates the flash drive may contain launch codes and the location of secret missile silos throughout Iraq and Iran—among other things—and each of the silos may be filled with rockets containing VX poison gas. All aimed, ready to fire directly onto Israel or their allies once the time is right."

Burke looked at Jones. He mumbled, "We're gonna need Mack on this trip."

Stallone heard Burke's words and said, "Already taken care of. He's on a plane as we speak. Get yourself to DC, gentlemen—and lady. A plane will be waiting for you. Once you land, we'll go over the plan about getting you in country."

"Roger that, sir," Burke said.

"Can't wait to get started," Lily piped up. "Let's go kill some bad guys. I mean. Stop. No thwart their evil plan." She gave an awkward virtual fist pound toward the screen.

Burke ignored the youthful quip about the terrorists and said, "We're on our way, sir."

CHAPTER FOUR

Burke sat in a conference room inside CIA headquarters in Langley. Everyone was there. Well, everyone except Stallone. Stallone was held up by a meeting, so as Burke and the others awaited his arrival, they all caught up with small talk. But Burke couldn't focus on Lily's story about hacking into the FBI's top ten list when she was only twelve. It all but faded away like a mist as his thoughts shifted to Naomi and their last mission together. Even with all of Naomi's shortfalls, deep down, Burke missed their relationship. And in the end, he forgave her for everything—mainly because she threw herself in front of a bullet to protect Burke's wife, Laura, and died in the process.

As Burke reminisced, he failed to see Stallone's entrance. It wasn't until Emily tapped him on the shoulder that he returned from his thoughts.

"Let's make this quick, shall we?" Stallone said. "We need to move on this now. I've just come from a debrief, and from what I've been told, it seems a terror group was moving in on V and Lopez, and chased them away from Damascus. Apparently, the two of them are trapped in some sort of abandoned hotel or office building. Some villagers in southern Syria offered them aid, and word got out to some insurgents over the border in Golan Heights, maybe ISIS, we don't know for sure. But now there is an imminent threat to their lives."

"What about the villagers?" Emily said.

"Overwatch tells us that some homes have been destroyed," Lily said. "And lives have been lost."

"So how do we know V and Lopez are even still alive?" Burke said. "Or if they still have the flash drive?"

"We don't have proof of life," Stallone said. "All we have to go on is the hope that they're still alive. No one has claimed responsibility for their capture, so they might not be yet. If, or when that takes place, we're expecting some kind of trade will be offered for their lives. However, at this point, we're still in the dark."

"What's the play here then?" Mack's excitement grew with each word. "Drop in from the sky? Take them in the night while they sleep?"

Emily laughed under her breath; there was no way that would be the plan.

"That's exactly the plan, Mack," Stallone said. "A HALO jump. High altitude, low open. It must be secret so no military radar can spot us."

Emily wore a look of shock and turned a lighter shade of pale. She and Burke hadn't got to that part of their training yet. They had only finished basic. Sure, she had jumped out of a plane with a friend in college for her birthday, but that was not a high-altitude jump. HALO jumps were dangerous. In fact, a HALO jump was by far the most dangerous jump that an operator can make from an aircraft. A lot can go wrong. With sometimes dire consequences.

"Nice," Mack said, bumping fists with Jones.

"We all know you'd rather jump from a perfectly good airplane than land in one," Burke teased his friend.

"What? Really? You're afraid to fly?" Lily had no idea.

"I am *not* afraid to fly." Mack beamed with pride.

"No, 'course not," Burke said. He winked at Lily, then whispered out of the corner of his mouth, "He's afraid to land."

Stallone cut them off. "All right, that's enough. Here's the plan." He pushed a button on the table, and the TV rose out of the center of it.

Burke stared at it as it rose. He couldn't help but think of the video Naomi had showed them before they left for Nigeria. The burned villagers in a charred heaped pile. Even though that mission turned out to be a success in the end, still, lives were lost. Lives that shouldn't have been lost. Burke and the others sat and watched as Lily went over their objective in this mission.

"This man is Saam Rajabi." A picture of Rajabi flashed across the screen. Then a video followed similar to the video Naomi had showed about President Kazah and his theoretical plots and exploits during his life of terror. "He was top priority for V and Lopez and the man we think is chasing them now. Their mission was to uncover his next target. They have been tracking him since 2020. Long before Hamas's attack on Israel last October. And it wasn't until only recently that they were able to uncover the link between Rajabi and the VX gas and their plans to eventually—when the time is right—strike. He's a zealot. Responsible for chaos throughout Syria, Lebanon, and parts of Iran. He's linked to thousands of casualties, more by my calculations. He's the absolute worst of the worst and our top priority."

"Wait, I thought top priority was rescuing V and Lopez?" Burke said.

Lily glanced over at Stallone and waited for him to speak.

"They are. But . . . we're preparing you for everything. If it ends up that V and Lopez are either already captured or get captured before you're able to get them out, this man is the one likely behind the abduction. The one you will have to deal with before the extraction."

"You mean his army of supporters," Mack said. "No way we get to him without a massive body count."

"Agreed," Stallone said. "That's why I'm sending you on this mission with backup."

Burke was taken aback. In all his years working for the agency, Naomi never sent him in with backup. Not ever. He had only worked alone or with Jones and Mack. Even Emily was new to the crew on their mission in Nigeria. More men seemed excessive. At the very least, more difficult to manage the egos.

"Backup?" Mack was brash and always had been. "Pssh. We don't need backup."

"I'm sending you in with a qualified strike team. We're collaborating with another special operations unit from the CIA. Three members. All former SEALs proficient in—"

"I'm gonna cut you off right there, slick," Burke said. "We know exactly what they're proficient in."

Not that Burke disliked the Navy—or the brave men and women who fought for them—it's just, each branch had their own pride when it came to special forces. Each thought their way of doing things was the best.

Stallone stifled his thoughts, while Burke found Jones's gaze. He had been unusually quiet during the briefing. Historically, Jones was the one who followed orders to a T.

"Where you at with this, Jonesy?" Burke said.

"Sounds like we're going into this half-cocked," Jones said.

"How so?" Stallone asked.

"Well, for starters—where is this Rajabi guy holed up? What does intelligence say?"

"Intelligence has him in Syria. His compound is north of Damascus. But recently he's moved south toward Israel."

"Okay, that tracks. So he's after our agents. No doubt trying to chase them down for this . . . this, thumb drive they stole—but what's his motivation?"

"What do you mean?" Stallone said.

"Lily said it herself. Rajabi's a zealot. And the only zealots I know are the ones willing to die for their cause. So, are we walking into a trap here? Like you say, he may be on to V and Lopez's position soon. If he comes out and makes a claim that he has them, whether we believe him or not, couldn't he be leading us into a trap? Maybe some random hotel or office building that he could just detonate upon our entering. Or even corner us with V and Lopez, then boom. Just to earn his spot in heaven with whatever deity he swears allegiance to."

"That *is* a possibility," Stallone said. "However, it's unlikely. The more likely scenario is that he will barter for their lives in exchange for . . ."

"For what?" Emily filled the silence.

"Money," Stallone said.

"There it is," Mack said.

"So, what, you're willing to directly fund terrorism?" Burke said.

"We've been doing it for years—why stop now?" Mack added. He didn't have proof but believed it to be true.

Stallone sighed. "If that's what it takes to get our people back, then yes. He is after all . . . a businessman."

"So you're willing to bet our lives on the fact that you know this zealot to be a businessman and only at this for the money?" Burke said.

Stallone swallowed hard. "Look, Burke, I don't like the play either, but you're the best of all Special Ops. I need you for this. We must get V and Lopez out of there. The hope is that you find them before Rajabi does, but if you can't, well, then we're going to have to improvise. Now, that's the order. Lily will be your eyes and ears from here in Langley. And the secondary team has already been briefed. You're meeting them on the tarmac in fifteen minutes to load up. So, prepare yourselves and make us proud." With that, Stallone exited the room.

Burke looked at Jones. Then over at Mack. Both nodded. They were ready. Then he shifted his eyes toward Emily. Her body language told the story: her head sank and her shoulders slouched as she grabbed the back of the leather chair in front of her.

Burke came over and put his hand on her shoulder. "You all right with this?" His question was rhetorical. He knew she wasn't. Not with the idea of a HALO jump. Even Burke wasn't sure about the mission. And something seemed off. Just the way Stallone was pushing the mission so fast, without much intelligence to go on or tactical assurances.

"Yeah," Mack said, chuckling, then continued painting the picture for her. "Imagine this. The rain on your skin. The moonlight on your face. The whipping wind blowing into your open mouth, causing you to almost drown on it. Just kidding. You won't feel any of that. This isn't some static jump where your chute deploys immediately. You'll have to protect your skin too. You know how cold it is at thirty thousand feet? And oxygen. It might fail on you, and you could lose consciousness and free-fall to your death."

"That's enough, Mack." Burke pushed his friend aside and shook his head. "Don't pay attention to him. He's just trying to get under your skin."

"Well, it's working." She gave him a sideways grin. Emily pushed away from the table and tried to catch her breath. "I don't know if I can do this, Burke?"

Burke stood tall. She was being honest; it was time for him to return the favor. "You're right, Emily. You're probably not ready for this."

She furrowed her brow. She wasn't expecting that kind of pep talk.

"But—and this I can tell you from experience—if you stay here out of fear and something happens to us over there, you'll second-guess your choice for the rest of your life."

She stared up at him, but there was fear in her eyes.

"And trust me," Burke continued, "you don't want that kind of regret on your conscience. No one does."

It didn't take her but a few seconds to come back. "You're right, Burke. The jump is too much. I'm not some special operator jonesing for terminal velocity—that's not me."

"So, what *is* you?"

"I'm going to get in country the old-fashioned way."

"How's that?" Lily chimed in.

"Covertly. Take the necessary connecting flights. Blend in. Use the skills both you and Naomi taught me over the years. Some of it has rubbed off," she said with a wink.

"You think Stallone will go for that?" Burke said.

"Who cares?" She turned her attention off Burke. "Lily, can you get your hands on a disguise kit for me?"

Lily shrugged. "Probably."

"Good. And maybe this way I'll be able to retrace V's steps. Figure out what exactly is on that flash drive." Emily turned toward Lily. "Can you get me her files too?"

"Could be above my clearance level for this mission, but . . ." Lily started.

"Get Stallone to sign off on it," Emily said. "If he wants V and Lopez back alive, then he'll get you what we need."

"You sure that's the route you want to take," Burke said. "Could be more dangerous than just jumping out of an airplane."

"That may be true, Burke. But this is what I know. Plus, I have former assets in the area I can call on if I get in a bind. Once I'm in country, we'll reestablish contact."

"That's what I'm talking about." Burke picked her up in a bear hug and spun her around.

Once he set her back down, Lily came close. "My turn. My turn."

Burke looked at her awkwardly, then lifted his hand for a high five. "Let's just start with this."

She smiled and smacked his hand. "I'll take it."

CHAPTER FIVE

Fifteen pieces of random objects were strewn across a table. Emily stood over the objects and made sure she had all the necessary items to aid her on her mission. Her legend, or her cover, was that of a reporter—not far from the truth. But her passport shows a different name, Emily Ryerson, not Kilpatrick. Easy enough to remember.

Her new persona, Emily Ryerson, was from a suburb of Minneapolis called Eden Prairie. Grew up on a nearby lake called Lake Riley. Her family wasn't rich, but they had all the necessities any child would love to have: a boat, trampoline in the backyard, large fire pit, two parents who loved her, and a bachelor's degree from the University of Minnesota in journalism. Emily Ryerson was the quintessential all-American girl. But that was her cover. And a story she would need to rehearse on the plane ride over.

Next to her fake passport were two hundred dollars in US currency in twenty-dollar increments, a pack of cigarettes, a lighter, a camera, and a notepad. That was all she was allowed to take with her. Anything else she needed she would have to obtain after her arrival.

"You ready for this?" Lily asked, tiptoeing into the room as Emily packed her reversible duffel bag.

Emily watched as Lily walked around the table to face her. "I am.

I'm used to this. Changing my name. Interacting with the locals. Blending in. That's what I've done for the better part of my adult life with the CIA."

"That's lit," Lily said without thinking.

"That's what?" Emily said.

"Oh, sorry, I mean, what you're doing—you're . . . it's just, well, I'd love to be in your shoes instead of behind a computer desk hacking satellites and spying on people. I'd rather be with you—with Burke—like the last mission. You know, where the action is."

Emily sighed. "I get it. You're young. Full of ambition. But trust me, there are times where I wish I had your skill set. To be able to stay here and work as an analyst. Sure, what I've done sounds exciting in theory, but I'd rather have not seen what I have seen. Some missions stay with you. And sometimes late at night, I can't turn off the images that plague my mind."

Just like that, Emily Kilpatrick began sounding like a CIA veteran. Quite the different feeling from years past.

"Ugh," Lily said. "Well, when you put it like that, being in the field sounds like a total buzzkill."

Emily laughed. "Sorry, didn't mean to taint your grandiose picture of what we do. But really, it's not that glamourous. It's just a job that needs doing. And in the end, the hope is to save lives."

"See, why didn't you just lead with that?"

Both women shared a laugh before Stallone walked in. They stifled their laughter and looked at him. He reached out and handed Emily a manila folder.

"These are the hard-copy files from V's findings on Rajabi. Read them before you leave Langley. Then return them to me."

Emily took the folder. "Thank you, sir."

He nodded. "There's a plane leaving from Dulles in two hours. Your ticket is inside. I want you on that plane."

She opened the folder and read the destination.

"Amman," she said aloud to herself. "Jordan?" Then she eyed Stallone.

"It's the safest airport nearest to V and Lopez's last known whereabouts."

"But Damascus is closer, sir—so is Beirut."

"But both cities are hostile territory for Westerners. You know that."

"Of course I do, but it's the fastest way into southern Syria."

"I get it, Emily. Just read the file. You may find that there are things in Jordan that need tending to. Assets V has used in the past. They will help you blend in."

Emily gazed at the floor as she considered his point.

"Lily, let's leave Emily to read the file. She needs to analyze and memorize everything before she leaves here. And she doesn't have much time."

Lily joined Stallone by the door, but before she left, she looked back at Emily. "I'll be watching you from here. If you need anything, don't hesitate to call."

"Yeah, yeah. Fine." Stallone ushered Lily out the door.

Once they were gone, Emily took the only chair in the room and pulled it up to the table. She set the file down and flipped it open. There were pictures inside. Pictures of V's principal—her target—Saam Rajabi. The pictures dated back to the late '90s when Rajabi was just a teenager. He was a low-ranking officer in Hamas's regime at the time.

Other photos were known associates of Rajabi. One named Cyrus stood out. He seemed to be pictured multiple times with Rajabi.

His bodyguard, Emily thought.

That seemed to track, even though, in the meeting with Burke and the others, they had not been briefed on Rajabi's known associates.

"What's your angle, Rajabi?" Emily questioned as she held her fingers to her temple. "Stallone said money, but I don't buy it."

The more Emily read into the situation, the more she sided with Jones and what he'd said before they left for the jump. "Half-cocked may have been right, Jonesy. This man looks like a zealot. Money may not satisfy his insatiable desire to eliminate all who oppose him." Jones second-guessed both the mission and Stallone's assessment of Rajabi's motivation. And Emily could tell that Burke had questions too. Even if he didn't make them known to Stallone.

Emily glanced at the circular analog clock above the door. She needed to get to the airport. Even though she could've read more in the file to nail down everything V had on Rajabi, she just didn't have the time.

She walked down the long corridor toward Stallone's office. When she arrived outside his door, she looked through the glass and saw that he was on the phone. Stallone showed Emily a finger and insisted she wait as he finished his call. Emily huffed and threw the file down at her side. Within ten seconds, he was off the phone and waved her inside.

"Did you find what you were looking for?"

"Enough to know that the man's a psycho, hell-bent on destroying his enemies."

"Then you've come to the same conclusion I and the others have."

"But you know as well as I do, sir, things aren't always what they seem."

"I can assure you, with Rajabi they are."

Emily swallowed the lump in her throat and set the file down. She wanted to say more, but she kept her thoughts about Rajabi and his motivations to herself. "Sir, I just have one question before I leave."

"What's that?"

"Why Veronica?"

"What do you mean?"

"I mean, why was V tasked with getting close to Rajabi? You said she's been after him since 2020."

"That's right."

"Well, why now? Why did she have to keep her cover that long? Why not move on him then?" Emily pointed at the folder. "From what it says in that file, you knew he was a high-ranking terrorist, worthy of the CIA, our military, or Homeland's attention. You could have gotten to him then. Maybe before he had access to the VX rockets. So, why wait?"

"That's more than one question, Emily."

She gritted her teeth and awaited an answer she knew wouldn't come.

"That's classified."

Emily threw up her hands and turned to leave. "Of course it is."

Stallone's words stopped her. "Did you see the last picture in the file?"

Emily stalled and looked down at the door handle. She hadn't. She had run out of time. She moved toward his desk and flipped open the file and riffled through the photos until she reached the final one.

"Her name is Natasha Zielinski."

Emily looked up at Stallone, then stared back at the photo to remember her. She was striking. Fair skinned. Thick brown eyebrows, pale blue eyes, a pointed nose, and full lips.

"She's with foreign intelligence and one of V's contacts in Amman. This is her last known address." Stallone passed Emily a piece of paper. "Commit it to memory. Then toss it. Find her. And find her fast. She may know where V and Lopez are hiding. Who knows how much time they have left."

CHAPTER SIX

THE CONSTANT WHITE NOISE OF THE CRUISING C-130 AT THIRTY thousand feet hummed in Burke's ears. As he lay back against the hard metal of the seat, he closed his eyes and went over the jump in his mind. It's something he had always done, ever since his first jump in Airborne School at Fort Benning, which is now Fort Moore. Now, more than a thousand jumps later, he still employed the very same ritual.

But as he closed his eyes, it wasn't the jump that plagued his mind; it was Emily's decision to stay behind. She was at ease with her decision, but Burke went over all the danger that could present itself as she made her way into Syria—especially during wartime.

"One minute until we're over the drop zone," the pilot's voice echoed inside Burke's helmet.

Burke opened his eyes and looked through his face shield. He saw Jones move toward the rear of the aircraft and open the rear cargo ramp to get into position for the jump.

The wind whipped inside the aircraft, and it was loud—even louder than the hum of the plane. He stared into the dark void of the night sky and sucked in a breath. He had never prayed before a jump of any kind—never saw the need—but this time something was compelling him. He felt the need to whisper a prayer, but he didn't know what to say. Nor did he know what to do. He folded his hands at first, then let them go. He closed his eyes again but thought that was too much. So he settled for saying the words in his mind.

Lord, protect me on this jump. Me and the others. And Emily, keep her safe too.

"Thirty seconds." The pilot's voice interrupted his thoughts.

Uh, amen.

Burke stood with the others. As they moved forward, Burke had a tinge of fear in his belly, always had on HALO jumps. People died on HALO jumps. Even special operators. Sure, it was a rare occasion, but it did happen.

"Fifteen seconds."

They stepped forward. Mack was first up. No one was going to take his lead spot. Behind Mack was Mathies Winston—otherwise known as Bear, an homage to Winnie the Pooh. Must have been his kids' favorite book. Maybe his own. The man didn't look like a bear. He was tall and lean. Maybe 185 or 190 pounds. But he was strong and fast. And he was the senior officer of the SEAL team that was there to assist Burke and the others.

Behind Bear was a guy named Jericho. He stood shorter than Bear, but he was wider. He was from Alaska originally. All Burke knew of the name Jericho was from what he'd randomly picked up from Bible stories. Burke had flipped through the Old Testament one day, only to happen upon Joshua 6. He read the passage and found the Israelites were able to conquer a city by marching around it while blowing trumpets and carrying the Ark of the Covenant. As Burke read the story, he thought it sounded like an odd movie scene. But history proved the words true even if he never understood the meaning.

Fourth in line was Sam Powell. Went by Sammy. A simple name for a simple man. He didn't say much after their brief meeting on the ground. And even Bear was quick to give a synopsis of his man.

"Sammy's a closed book," Bear had said. "Don't ask him about his life. No one knows where he came from or what he did before he joined up."

Then it was Jones. Finally, Burke.

"Now or never, boys," the pilot said, "Go, go, go."

Burke watched as Mack fell first into the dark sky. He didn't even hesitate at the command. And with each succeeding man stepping forward to jump, Burke mirrored their movements. Before Jones leaped, he reached back and bumped fists with Burke. Something they did for good luck.

Jones walked over the edge of the ramp, and Burke followed closely. He opened his arms wide to brace himself against the wind. Falling in the dark of night was something Burke had never fully gotten used to—like night diving in the ocean. Not that diving or jumping from a plane was any different during the day—the instruments all reacted the same. But the unknown of things unseen was something Burke had struggled with; he had to learn to shut off the fear that came with the lack of light.

Against the whipping wind Burke stabilized himself. The freefall from thirty thousand feet typically lasted almost two full minutes, and they needed to deploy their parachutes above three thousand feet. If they deployed their parachutes at less than that, there was a greater risk for injury if there was any problem or an entanglement.

Burke glanced at the glowing altimeter on his wrist and saw that he was approaching four thousand feet. "C'mon, Jonesy. Pull the cord," Burke said to himself as he watched beneath him hoping Jonesy would deploy early and he might pass by.

He couldn't see much as he approached, but soon he saw the shadow of Jones's chute in the darkened sky. Burke was too close to him, however, and he was falling fast and directly toward Jones's open chute. Burke made a tactical move in the air, tucking his arms to his side to propel forward like a rocket to avoid Jones in midair. Unfortunately, his rucksack shifted on his back and threw him off balance. The move ripped his oxygen mask from his face shield and Burke was in a tailspin. He had to get under control, or he would fall below three thousand feet in a matter of seconds. Fortunately, Burke did not need the oxygen mask at their current altitude, but still he spun.

He was at 3,235 feet and falling fast.

He reached back and tickled the rip cord with his fingertips. He yanked hard and braced for impact. Nothing happened. The chute did not deploy beyond his pack. The cord was tangled, and he was in a dead spin. Burke's heart was in his throat, but he had to remain calm in the height of uncertainty.

He only had one other option: his last resort was to pull the cutaway and deploy his reserve chute. As he whipped around in circles, he reached back against the spin, grabbed hold of the chord, and for the second time in a matter of minutes, he prayed.

CHAPTER SEVEN

A DIM LIGHTBULB SWAYED OVERHEAD. IT FLICKERED FOR A FEW seconds before going completely dark. The bulb wasn't dying, it was just that the electricity in the building was volatile, turning the lights on and off at random. Two people sat facing each other on metal chairs in the middle of the room. They were bound, gagged, their faces beaten. They weren't alone, but neither could see the man standing in the corner, hiding in the shadows, who'd terrorized them only moments before.

Rajabi glanced down at his phone and read a text that came through with information regarding one of the operatives. When he looked back up, his eyes had to adjust to the constant flashing of the bulb. The strobing effect annoyed him, but he didn't stifle it. He knew that it helped to heighten the level of fear in both the man and the woman, who sat slouched in their chairs.

Most of his men waited outside and stood guard by the door—everyone except Cyrus. Cyrus was the one who'd doled out the beating that caused the man and woman so much pain. Two minutes of constant pounding. As Rajabi watched, he was surprised by their strength. The ability of both to endure such a beating and remain quiet about the whereabouts of the flash drive was inspiring. But Rajabi had a different kind of inspiration in mind.

Rajabi appeared from obscurity and stepped in front of them as they sat, hoping the new information would get them to spill their guts. When the next flash of light came, he made his presence known.

"I'll ask again, where is the flash drive?"

The man raised his head slowly and turned toward him. Rajabi stared at his swollen eye. He exaggerated a wince of pain at the sight of it. Then he shifted his gaze from the man and moved toward the woman. Her head was down. Tears mixed with blood and sweat streamed down her delicate face.

Cyrus circled the man and ripped out his gag so he could speak. The man continued to sit and offered no response to Rajabi's line of questioning.

Cyrus swung around and stood directly behind the woman. He stood over her and stared down at the man. The man took his eye off Rajabi and watched Cyrus as he towered over the woman. Cyrus reached down and untied her gag. She spat it out, then forced out a cough that led into a dry heave.

Cyrus reached forward and grabbed a head full of her hair and yanked backward, revealing her throat as he ran his hand down her long neck. Then he brought his knife toward her and dug the tip of the blade into her flesh. The sharpness of the edge pierced her skin, and a drop of blood appeared around the tip.

"Don't touch her," the man seethed through gritted teeth as he pulled at his bindings.

Rajabi stepped forward and bent down to the man's level. "This can all end now if you tell me where the flash drive is."

The man stared at him. "We already told you. We don't know what you're talking about."

Rajabi raised up and turned his back on the man. "Nice try, Mr. Lopez." It was the first time Rajabi had used his name. When Rajabi turned back around, Lopez looked somewhat shocked. "I know that you and Ms. Alberts have been tracking me since earlier this year. Maybe longer. And I know you stole from me. You stole the flash drive. I'm not sure if you know entirely what is on that flash drive, but if you don't return it to me, then, well . . ." He trailed off. "I'm afraid I'm going to unleash Cyrus on your friend."

Cyrus grinned wide.

"I promise, he won't be as gentle as before on you . . . you or your family."

The look of shock washed over Lopez's face. Rajabi had never made mention of his family.

"That's right." Rajabi looked down at his phone and read off the text message he had received only moments earlier. "Gilberto Cerarra." It was his real name, not his CIA cover. "And you have two daughters, a son, and a wife named Camilla. That's correct?" Rajabi's didn't expect an answer. "I have the address too. Someplace in Georgetown. Stop me if I'm wrong about any of this."

Lopez's mouth hung open. He wondered how Rajabi had access to that information.

"Don't be so surprised. We have many people staged in your government to do exactly this. I would've used this tactic with Veronica, too, but she has no known living relatives."

"What do you want?" Lopez spit some blood out when he spoke.

"You know exactly what I want. Give me the location of the flash drive."

Veronica perked up and said, "And once we do, you'll kill us both."

"If you don't, I'll have my man in the US kill every one of Lopez's family members. And if you think what Cyrus did to you here was bad, just use your imagination on what my man will do to your wife and children."

Rajabi watched Lopez stare at Veronica. They didn't break eye contact. Tears continued to fall from her eyes and also from his.

"So, what do you say, Mr. Lopez? Will you spare your wife and children the pain? Or are you willing to put them, you, and Ms. Alberts through more torment?"

Lopez lowered his head in shame. "Okay."

"Lopez, no—you can't," Veronica said, but Cyrus closed her mouth with a hard slap.

Lopez continued. "We hid the flash drive in a building when you caught on to us. One that we had in play for weeks. One we knew we could access at any part of the day due to its current state."

"And what state is that?"

"It's under construction and unoccupied."

"Lopez, please stop," Veronica pleaded with him.

But Lopez couldn't stop; he was too afraid for his family.

"Go on," Rajabi said.

"And the building is rigged to blow."

"Rigged to blow how?"

"We have another asset watching the building on a live feed."

"So what happens if someone enters the building?"

Lopez lifted his head and grinned as if he somehow had the power in that line. "If it's not me and V together, she'll blow it up."

Rajabi digested the story. He wondered if he could fully believe the yarn Lopez was spinning. "Why go to all the trouble with an abandoned building? Why not hide the flash drive in some . . . safety deposit box?"

"Is that where you keep your money?" Lopez quickly replied. "In some random bank in the middle of Syria? Not the most trusting of places, especially for Westerners."

Rajabi continued to listen and work the story through in his mind. It made sense. He did not keep his money in a bank anywhere near there.

"So, where is *this* building?" Rajabi said.

Before Lopez could answer, Veronica cut him off. "There's just one problem with the ending to that story."

Rajabi narrowed his eyes. "What's that?"

"I made a copy of the flash drive."

"You did what?" Rajabi stood over her and reared his open hand, but she didn't budge. She was tough, and the time for flinching at his ego was over.

"I made a copy of the flash drive," she repeated.

"And where is this alleged copy?"

"I don't have it on me, but it's close."

"How close?" Rajabi said.

"Minutes away," Veronica took her eyes off Rajabi and stared at Lopez. Lopez looked dumbfounded.

Rajabi reached behind her and cut her bindings. Then Lopez's.

"Take me there. And don't even think about trying to cross me, because now you know what kind of man I am."

CHAPTER EIGHT

THE GROUND WAS CLOSING IN ON BURKE, BUT HE WAS NO LONGER falling at over two hundred miles per hour. After a strong yank on the cord, his reserve chute deployed like it should have, and now he was hovering only a few hundred feet above the ground. That was close. Too close. In the moonlight he saw what was most likely deep shades of green as he approached. Probably trees. Then there was a contrast of a lighter shade. He recognized this lighter shade as the ground. How rocky it might be, he had no clear idea.

Their drop point was just outside an agricultural village. That's where further intelligence had V and Lopez located. Burke furrowed his brow and strained to see the ground. He braced himself by pulling his knees up, but he could only react out of instinct.

When he hit the rocky terrain, a jolt of pain ran through his shins and led up his legs until the pain reached his hips. There was a crunch, and Burke felt it. Getting older was not easy on the bones. Especially when jumping from over thirty thousand feet. His body no longer recovered the same way it did in his twenties—or even early thirties. This type of operation was starting to take its toll on Burke's aging body.

Once on the ground, Burke dropped his rucksack off his shoulder and ripped out his night-vision goggles. After putting them over his eyes, everything went a light shade of green. He saw someone, but he couldn't tell who it was from his position. Only that they were rummaging through their own rucksack. Burke stared east and saw dim lights—like the small village had some semblance of life at this early morning hour. Then he looked to his west, nothing but vast darkness amongst the mountainous terrain. Burke tore out his earpiece and stuck it in his ear.

Midsentence, Burke heard Mack saying, "Burke, you there? You copy?"

"I'm here. Just hit the ground."

"You okay?" Jones said. "Saw you pass by me in a flat spin."

"You know me—I'm always good," Burke said, but even he hadn't known if he was going to make it out of that spin alive. "Everyone accounted for?"

Each man called out his own name. All were on the ground and ready to march.

"Good," Burke said. "Make for the rendezvous point. We push from there."

The rendezvous point was a point marked on the map before the jump. No more than two clicks from Burke's position. He studied his location device and used his compass to move forward.

Just ahead of him, Burke found Jones. "Jonesy."

"I'm here, Burke."

They joined each other in their forward pursuit. Each man hoofed it fast but kept an eye out for enemy combatants. From their position the enemy could be hiding anywhere. There were trees all around. More buildings to the east and deeper into Syria to the north, which was controlled by any number of rebel forces. Not an ideal location for extraction, which made Burke question the rescue mission altogether.

After a 1.2-mile hike through the wilderness, Burke and the others encountered no resistance. Burke stopped at a tree line that paralleled a street. They stopped and used it for cover. Across the road was a three-story building. Was it abandoned? Likely. That's what intel suggested. It certainly looked dilapidated. Worn down by time. But Burke and the others had seen far worse buildings in that part of the world used for housing—so he was not about to judge any structure based on outward appearance.

If it was the building V and Lopez were being held in, Burke expected to see some opposition, some form of soldierly pushback, but there was none. Not one man standing guard.

"This is strange, Burke," Jones said.

"Tell me about it. Not what I expected to see."

"Maybe this isn't the right building," Bear said.

Burke recalled their debrief. Could they have missed their drop zone? Sure. Could this be the wrong farming community? Maybe. Burke didn't know how many agricultural villages there were in southern Syria, but there was no way of knowing if this was the right place until they cleared the building for the enemy.

"We move as one unit. Clear each room before moving on to the next," Bear declared.

Burke knew that would be the SEALs' plan of attack. And it wasn't wrong. But Burke wanted eyes on the back of the building and the roof to make sure they weren't walking into a trap, like Jones had suggested from the outset.

"Before we do, let me take a look at the building from another angle," Burke said.

Burke reached inside his pack and took something out. During his time in Special Reconnaissance, he was adept at finding moles inside the cracks. And part of his job was surveillance intelligence and using small, unmanned aircraft, or drones. The drone—which was no bigger than Burke's hand—could give them a vantage point none had from their current position.

"That thing is sick," Jericho said.

"Not something you SEALs are used to seeing, huh?" Mack puffed out his chest.

"No. That's not a toy we have at our disposal," Bear said.

"You won't believe the clarity on this camera too," Burke said.

Burke lifted the drone into the air, and then took control of the flight through his handheld device. He flew the drone higher in the sky than he needed to, to see around all sides of the building. He needed to keep anyone who might be standing guard from hearing the gentle buzz of the drone, especially in the stillness of night. The controlling device looked like any eight-inch tablet, except for the fact that it had a three-inch antenna at the top.

The men gathered around Burke as he flew the drone. The clarity was near perfect, even better than their night-vision goggles. It would also pick up movement with thermal imaging. Burke lifted the drone over the roof. Not one man stood post there. This seemed odd. It would have been a perfect place to hide. You would have a high vantage point and likely see the enemy coming from any direction.

Burke kept flying the drone around the entire perimeter. On the opposite side of the building, they noticed the first sign of movement. Two men, potentially military, were surveying the area. They had weapons. Possibly automatic rifles.

"That's two," Burke mumbled to the group in case anyone missed what he saw.

As Burke continued to fly the drone, he saw no more men guarding the building. He made one more pass, then returned the drone. Mack reached out his hand, and Burke landed it perfectly in his palm.

"I say we take out the two men before we enter the building," Bear said. "Again, work as two three-man teams. I'll take post with one of yours, and you take one of mine. Burke, you can come up from the rear to watch our six."

"Mack, you go with Bear," Burke nodded.

"Sammy, you hang back with Burke and Jones," Bear instructed his man.

Sammy nodded. Each man took his position. Bear stood up and ran across the street first. Jericho and Mack were on his heels. They eyed both ends of the street. Then Bear said, "Clear."

Burke and the others followed the same path, and as Bear made his way toward the corner of the building, Burke kept his M4 pointed in the opposite direction. Every man was skilled in warfare and knew how to locate any threat. They never stayed in the same spot long. Always moving.

The corner was close. Bear stopped and allowed Burke's group to move tighter. Just as Burke's group caught up, Jericho reached out and squeezed Bear's shoulder to let him know that backup had arrived.

As Bear peered around the corner of the building, the first shots rang out in the dead silence of night.

CHAPTER NINE

Bear dropped the man on the side of the building with one shot. "One down," he said into the earpiece.

Burke and the others rounded the corner and worked as one unit. As they came upon the fallen man, Burke glanced down at Bear's handiwork. The shot was perfectly placed in the center of his head. *Not bad,* Burke thought.

He came upon the next corner of the building. From Burke's drone reconnaissance, it looked as if one man was covering either side of the building.

Bear stalled at the edge and gave Burke's team a moment to catch up. Jericho squeezed Bear again on the shoulder. Bear turned the corner with his rifle pointed out, but there was no shot to be taken.

Burke couldn't see what Bear saw, not until he rounded the corner himself. Burke peered down the long stretch but saw no sign of another man.

Where is he? Burke thought.

The only move for the remaining man would've been to retreat into the building, maybe alert others of shots fired. At least that's what Burke would've done.

A doorway ahead led inside the building. Bear stopped and waited with his group of three. They took a knee near the door and waited until Burke's crew caught up. Burke's group kneeled opposite the door frame. Bear reached for the handle and pushed the door inward.

Burke peered through his scope and watched for any sign of movement. The others did the same. Bear slowly pushed through the opening. Jericho and Mack followed on his heels. Then Burke, Jones, and Sammy.

The room they entered was an atrium. Not something Burke and the others expected to see, especially in the middle of a random farming community. The two-story glass atrium was more befitting a larger city. Maybe Damascus. Or some grand hotel. The room was wide open, not the preferred way for a tactical team to enter a building. Too many open sight lines. Too many areas of concern. Too many opportunities for an ambush. They needed to get out of there and fast.

Bear rushed across the open area, then found a closed door across the lobby. Burke continued to watch Bear's six. He was shocked they weren't meeting any resistance.

Once Burke caught up, Bear reached out and pushed the door open, which led him into a meeting space. The chairs were scattered, and some of the tables were overturned. They spread out inside the smaller space, guns raised.

As Burke's team moved right, Burke could hear faint whispers coming from the opposite side of the room, and just as he walked past the first overturned table, a man jumped up from the back of the room and opened fire. Burke shouldered his rifle and returned fire—as did the remaining five. One of the shot bursts caught the man and sent him to the floor. Burke and the others continued to check the room for other threats.

Burke reached the fallen man first. He was bloodied, shot three times in the middle of the chest and once in the gut. The man had but a few remaining seconds left on earth as Burke hovered over him. He noticed a walkie-talkie lying next to the man's open hand.

"Where are they?" Burke said. "The American journalists—where are they being held?"

The man struggled to laugh, but blood was in his throat and clogged his airway.

Mack caught up and forced his rifle close to the man's head—as if that was going to intimidate him; the man's fate was already sealed. Why would he say anything in the last remaining moments of his life?

"Save your threats, Mack," Burke said. "He's not gonna tell us anything."

"Do you think this is the other guy we saw on the drone footage?" Bear said.

Burke nodded. "I do."

"Where are the others?" Jericho said.

Burke turned his head to the side. "Maybe on the other end of the walkie-talkie."

"Why come inside and hide?" Jericho said. "Why not bring down everything they have on us? I mean the hall back there was a death box. Can't believe we made it out of there alive."

Jericho, Bear, and Sammy shared a laugh, but Jones cut in. "Because no one else is here."

They all turned to him.

"What do you mean, Jonesy?" Burke said.

"I mean, Rajabi. His men. No one else is here. Bet you a hundred we don't find a single soul left in this building." Jones nodded at the man on the floor. "My guess . . . this guy and the guy outside were left behind."

"I'll take that bet," Jericho said.

"What about if we find Lopez or V upstairs dead?" Mack added.

Bear was taken aback. "Easy, Mack. Let's have some respect here."

"What?" Mack shrugged. "I'm not saying I want that to happen. I'm just trying to get clarification on the rules of the wager. I'm not looking at getting swindled here."

Bear scrunched his brow. Still, he didn't know how to take Mack's response.

Burke leaned into Bear's space. "He means no offense," Burke said. "That's just who he is."

Bear ignored Burke's explanation. "Let's just clear the rest of the building and get out of here. Never know if Rajabi's men will be coming back."

"Roger that."

Bear broke away with Jericho and Mack, but before they were fully away, Bear looked over at Mack and said, "Stay frosty. Contrary to popular belief, there may be more threats in the building, so don't let your guard down."

Mack peered over his shoulder and eyed Burke. Without saying a word, he told Burke everything. Burke grinned at his friend. He knew Mack found it laughable that Bear thought they needed tactical advice.

As they worked their way through the building, they checked each room on the first floor, then moved on to the second. Most of the second floor was empty office space. It wasn't until they reached the third floor that they found the winner of Jones's little bet.

No one was there.

The third floor was completely unfinished. No walls. No sheetrock. Nothing, except for two folding chairs in the middle of the room beneath a lone lightbulb. The two teams worked their way over toward the chairs. They were empty. Burke bent down to the floor to examine two strands of rope long enough to tie hands and feet. The bindings were cut.

"I got something over here on the floor," Sammy said. His first words since they got on the ground.

"Oh, he does speak," Mack teased.

They walked over to see Sammy pointing his rifle and his flashlight toward the dirty floor.

"Blood," Burke said.

As Sammy continued moving his flashlight, Burke lifted his head and found Bear.

"That's blood, all right," Bear added.

"They were here." Burke turned back toward the chairs.

"And didn't leave that long ago," Jericho said, bending down to run his fingers over the stain. "This blood is still wet."

"Question is . . . ," Burke started, "where are they now?"

CHAPTER TEN

Cyrus sped west down the two-lane road away from the village. Rajabi's crew of five other vehicles followed close behind in their version of a convoy.

"Where is it?" Rajabi leaned into V's face in the backseat of the SUV. "Where's the flash drive?"

Veronica leaned away from him to avoid the spit that came along with his shout.

"V, tell him. Think of my family." Lopez could only react out of fear. Rajabi smashed him across the face with the butt of his handgun as he sat in the third row.

"You keep your mouth shut, boy. No more talking from you. It's her turn to talk."

Rajabi reengaged with Veronica just as he lowered himself back down into his seat. He straightened his shirt and waited for her to give Cyrus more direction other than, "Head west."

Veronica dropped her chin to the floor. "Not far. In the next village. In a nearby cemetery," she said.

Cyrus knew precisely the cemetery she was talking about. He pushed his foot down on the gas pedal, and it took only five minutes to arrive.

"Park at the south entrance," Veronica said.

Rajabi hit his man on the shoulder from the backseat and pointed ahead. "There's a spot there. Take it."

The driver obeyed. The entrance to the cemetery looked like any cemetery would. There was a memorial dedicated to fallen soldiers from the local area. There were thick grass and mature trees, although both were hard to see in the dark. The trees looked like shadows against the night sky watching over the graves. It was well lit in places, but others not so much—which was going to make the hunt for the flash drive difficult.

Fifteen more men stepped out of the vehicles and faced Rajabi. He spoke to them in Persian and told them to spread out. Each man had his own duty—his own post for protection. Once his men dispersed, Rajabi aimed his gun at Veronica and said, "We're here. Now where is it?"

Veronica looked at Lopez. He was bent over, holding his gut. He winced in pain from the beating he'd taken in the hotel and was still coughing to catch his breath.

"It's close by," she said.

"What are you waiting for then? Move!" Rajabi said.

"I'll need a flashlight."

Cyrus lifted one from his pocket and handed it to her. She flicked the switch, turned around, and walked north. There was a grouping of trees they had to push through before they reached the first grave site.

Rajabi followed close behind—his eyes danced, and his head was on a swivel. He knew she could be leading him into a trap.

She walked and walked. It seemed like forever, but that could've been because it was dark and difficult to navigate the undulating ground of the cemetery. She stopped on three occasions to shine her light on a headstone. On the fourth, Rajabi lost his cool.

"Where is it?" He made up the difference between himself and her.

She cowered and lowered her head. "I know it's . . ." She was stalling. "It . . . has to be here someplace." She spun in a circle, like she was still searching for the right spot.

"I'm growing tired of your games, Ms. Alberts." Rajabi raised his gun and pointed it at her.

She held up her hands. "No, it's here. I swear. Please don't kill me."

"You have one more chance. The next time you stop, if it's not for the flash drive"—Rajabi lowered his gun from her chest and pointed it at Lopez—"you're going to cause him more pain."

She shook her head furiously. "Please. Stop. No. Lower your gun."

She stepped toward Rajabi. Then he aimed his gun back at her.

"Move."

She scanned the area with the flashlight. She shined the beam on the exterior rock wall. Near the wall were over a dozen headstones. Planted in front of the headstones were tiny trees that hadn't had time yet to mature.

"It's there." She pointed to the ground.

"Where?" Rajabi said.

"Under that tree."

Rajabi shined his own flashlight at Veronica and said, "What are you waiting for? Dig."

Veronica dropped to her knees. She had no shovel, only her hands. Lopez dropped to the ground next to her, and they began to tear at hardened dirt with their fingernails.

Rajabi watched them dig until one of his men who was on patrol called out in the night. "I see someone."

Rajabi went rigid, and Cyrus stepped in front of him and pulled him behind his back to shield off any threat. Rajabi's man stared northeast, back toward the direction they'd come from. There was nothing but a small collection of trees about twenty yards away, and then the elevation fell off into a dark empty chasm.

"It's nothing," the man came back. "Just an animal."

Rajabi sighed, then turned back around. Both Veronica and Lopez had taken off on foot, running west toward the road.

"Get them," Rajabi called out to his men.

All abandoned their patrols to track down Veronica and Lopez, which wouldn't prove too difficult because both were injured. Once they were caught, one man held on to the back of Veronica's hair and the other gripped Lopez.

Rajabi walked up to Veronica, leaned close and said, "The flash drive is not here, is it?"

She did not speak. Her silence told him everything he needed to know.

Rajabi nodded. "I see how this is going to go." He needed to heighten their level of fear, so he stood up straight and walked directly over to Lopez. He reared up and hit Lopez on the back of the head with the butt of his pistol and knocked him out cold. Then he raised the barrel as he lay on the ground and opened fire.

CHAPTER ELEVEN

Burke lifted his satellite phone and called Langley. The number went directly to Lily.

"Was wondering when I'd hear from Captain America," Lily said.

Burke smiled but didn't have time to chitchat or get his ego stroked. "We need your help."

"I figured that's why you called. What's up?"

"We need to find Rajabi. He's not here. We're inside the building—the one we went over during the debrief. We're on the third floor, and it looks like this is where V and Lopez were being held, except—" Burke cut himself off.

"Except what?" Lily said.

"Except for cut pieces of rope and blood on the floor."

"On it," Lily said. Then she mumbled to herself, and Burke could hear her banging away on her computer. "Okay, got it. I have them on CCTV escaping the building in a convoy. Looks like . . ." She paused a moment. Burke heard more typing. "Maybe five or six vehicles. They headed south and west from your position."

"Headed southwest," Burke said off the phone to the rest of the team.

"Correct. I'll see if I can find any more CCTV footage and then get back to you."

The men readied their guns. "Stay together. We leave as one unit," Bear said.

"Thanks for your help, Lily," Burke said as he followed Bear out of the room. "I'll be in touch soon—"

"Wait, Burke, before you go."

"What is it?" Burke said.

"I wanted to let you know that Emily is on a plane. Headed for Amman, Jordan."

"Amman?" Burke questioned. "Why Amman?"

"Stallone figured that was the safest airport closest to where you are."

"Yeah, I guess that makes sense. Considering her only other option would be Damascus or Beirut. When is she scheduled to land?"

"Midmorning. Like ten, I think."

"Roger that. Thanks again, Lily."

Burke ended the call and proceeded down the staircase in the same formation that they took the building in. This time, though, they didn't linger long to search each floor. And once they reached the main level, Bear moved toward the fallen man they had shot upon entering. They needed a vehicle, and it was likely he or the other dead man had access to one. They also might have intelligence on them about Rajabi. Maybe something to clue them in about his plans after finding the flash drive.

Burke and the four others surrounded Bear as he searched the body—each man with his eye and rifle ready for attack from any direction.

After a few moments of searching, Jericho spoke over his shoulder. "Find anything?"

After a few moments, Bear threw his hands up and cursed under his breath.

"What?" Burke said.

"Guy's got nothing. Not even a stick of gum in his pockets."

The group let out a grunt. Then Burke said, "Let's move outside and check the other one. Maybe he's got something we can use."

After working their way through the atrium, they took the back entrance and headed toward the man outside. Burke reached him first, took a knee, then dug through the man's possessions. Burke reached into his fatigue pockets and felt the unmistakable rigid edge of a key. He grabbed the key and ripped it out of his pocket.

"Got 'em." He found Jones's eyes first.

"Now we just have to find the vehicle," Jones said.

"And hope it fits six jacked dudes and all their gear," Mack said.

Burke chuckled at Mack's joke, but then realized Mack spoke truth. Burke hoped it was big enough for them as well.

Bear suddenly yelled out, "Contact! Twelve o'clock!"

Shots were fired from a car that had stopped up the alleyway about eighty feet from their position. They were bogged down and only had two options: shoot until the threat is neutralized or retreat into the atrium. In their current position they had no cover. Staying in the alleyway would have been suicide.

Burke and the others backed out of the firefight and withdrew inside the building.

"Split up," Bear was quick to say once they were inside. "Move upstairs . . . there . . . and there." He pointed to the staircases on opposite sides. "Stay in your teams. We'll have the advantage from an elevated position."

Burke ran toward the flight of stairs. Jones and Sammy were right behind him. When Burke reached the second level, he looked across the atrium to see Bear, Jericho, and Mack split apart and stack their rifles on the railing that they used as cover and point their guns at the only entrance they could see. Burke, Jones, and Sammy mirrored their movements.

The sound of his heart echoed in Burke's ears. He closed his eyes and sucked in a deep breath to slow down his breathing. He calmed his elevated rate just as the first threat presented itself. Burke took aim and was just about to squeeze the trigger, but something caught his eye on the back side of the atrium—another man. And he posed a much bigger threat, one that was directed right at Bear, Jericho, and Mack—and not one of them saw it.

"*RPG*," Burke yelled and fired off a round from his rifle.

As the rocket-propelled grenade was headed directly for his friends, Burke's bullet was headed for the enemy.

The explosion lit up the darkness and turned their green night vision into a burst of bright light. Burke yanked the goggles from his face and stared toward the fire. He saw no movement from anyone.

Bullets continued to fly toward him. He dropped to the floor and heard Jones and Sammy return fire toward the first floor below. Burke backed against the second-floor balcony, and once his vision returned to normal, he put his night-vision goggles back over his eyes. Two more men had entered. Burke fired at them, as did Jones and Sammy, but no shots came from Bear, Jericho, and Mack's location.

Once the two enemies fell, there was a pause in gunfire. Burke didn't know if the threat had been eliminated, and he wasn't about to stand up and lift his rifle.

After thirty seconds of silence, Burke took a look through his scope, toward the opposite side of the atrium. Still no movement. No sign of Bear, Jericho, or Archie Mack, one of his best friends in the entire world.

CHAPTER TWELVE

BURKE'S EYES WERE STUCK WIDE OPEN. HE REACHED OUT FOR Jones's arm and pulled it down. "Have you seen any movement? Mack, the others . . . have you seen them since the . . ." Burke trailed off and raised his neck to see over the railing.

He already knew the answer to his own question, but he wanted reassurance. Jones shook his head no. Then Burke looked at Sammy. He did the same. Immediately, Burke turned toward the staircase.

"Burke, wait," Jones said. "We need to stay put. Be smart. There could be more of them."

But he didn't.

"*Burke*!"

Burke didn't care about the possibility of another threat; he needed to find Mack and the others and make sure they were still breathing.

He ran down the staircase and sprinted across the courtyard without waiting for backup. His focus was resolute. With the coast clear, he reached the staircase and looked upward. The explosion had blown up the ceiling of the second floor. The staircase remained undamaged, and from Burke's recollection, Mack and the others were at least fifteen feet away from the top of the stairs.

Debris was everywhere. Glass. Brick. Wood. Plaster. All mixed in a heaped pile.

"*Mack*," Burke called out.

There was a muffled groan ahead of him. Then the sharp screech of a boot. Burke whipped around and saw Jones climbing the stairs to join him. Sammy stayed put to cover their backs as they searched.

"Mack. Bear. Jericho. You there?" Burke said.

There was movement ahead of him and an arm raised through the pile of rubble. Burke recognized Mack's gloves. Always wore the same brand. A drab, muted brown.

"Mack! That you?"

Mack closed his fist and turned his thumb upward. Burke grinned. Apparently, Mack wasn't taking his situation too seriously. Burke slung his rifle around his back and bent down to help get rid of the remnants that covered his friend.

Once Mack's face was revealed, he said, "Well, that sucked."

Burke laughed. "Could've been a lot worse."

Mack pulled himself the rest of the way out and stood to his feet.

"Any sign of Bear or Jericho?" Jones said.

Mack pointed. "Jericho was there. And Bear was up another ten feet or so."

The walk forward was more difficult to navigate. They heard another grunt. Suddenly, Jericho burst through the debris like a great white shark exploding through the surface for a dying seal. He took a deep breath and aimed his rifle in all directions. He was frantic, as if he'd just regained consciousness. Once he caught eyes with Burke and the others, he calmed his heavy breathing.

"What happened?" he said.

"RPG. Took down the floor above us." Mack pointed toward the ceiling.

Jericho looked up to see the gaping hole in the second-story floor.

"Damn. Close call," Jericho said.

"You can say that again," Mack said, then turned toward Burke and Jones. "Speaking of, how'd he miss?"

"Who?" Jericho cut in.

"Who?" He glared back at Jericho. "The kid selling cookies downstairs," Mack mocked, scrunching his brow and shaking his head. "The guy firing the RPG. Why did he take out the ceiling above us and not the floor below us for a direct hit?"

"'Cause Burke shot him," Jones quipped back.

"Seriously?" Mack said.

Burke nodded. He was reluctant to take too much credit. Anyone would've done the same thing in his position.

"Wasn't a tough shot," Burke said with a shrug. "He was focused on that big ole head of yours."

Mack laughed. "Yuk it up. At least my big head is still attached. I'm fine chalking that up to owing you my life one more time, Burke." Mack nudged him.

"Where's Bear?" Jericho broke up the ego fest and found his footing.

"*Bear*," Burke yelled.

"Shh." Jones moved his hand up and down to quiet him down. "We don't know if there's anyone else outside."

"Where are you, buddy?" Jericho did not heed his warning. In fact, neither had Burke when he came looking for Mack. When you serve with men—especially men in the same unit on multiple tours—they become like family. And damn the consequences. You'll do whatever it takes to find them when they're missing. Alive or dead.

After about two minutes of searching, they found Bear. Burke lifted the last remaining piece of debris off him to reveal a shard of metal jammed into the center of his chest—right through the heart.

Burke's head fell, and breath left his body. It could have easily been Mack, Jones, or even himself. But it was Bear's time to die and not his, only God knows why. Burke gave up trying to understand that mystery. He'd always heard people say it was just luck or God's plan, but he didn't know how to reconcile that in his own head. At least not in the past. However, after what he'd seen, read, and felt at the soul level lately, the veil was starting to lift. He was beginning to see more clearly. But still . . . it never made the death of a friend or man you served with any easier.

Jericho seethed in anger and pounded the floor. "Get him out of here. We're not leaving him—he's coming with us."

"There was never a doubt," Burke said. "Mack. Help Jericho with Bear's legs." Burke turned over his shoulder and spoke to Jones. "Take these keys." Burke handed him the set he'd taken off the other man. "Or see if you can find any keys on the men downstairs. Take Sammy with you. Try to find a vehicle while I check in with Lily. See if she has any more intel on Rajabi's location."

"Copy that."

Burke lifted his satellite phone and called Lily. She answered right away.

"Burke, that you?"

"Who else?"

"Well, I have been getting a lot of spam calls lately, so you just never know," she said with a giggle.

With Bear gone, Burke wasn't about to laugh at her meager attempt at a joke.

"Sheesh, I thought that was a bit clever. Not even a courtesy chuckle?"

"Now's not the time, Lily. Bear's dead."

"Dead? What? Burke—how?"

"Shrapnel from an RPG explosion."

"That's . . . that's . . ." She trailed off.

"Yeah, it sucks. What'd you find on CCTV?"

"I'm sorry."

"Unfortunately, it's part of the job. Let's move forward."

"Okay, uh, yeah . . . I just tracked the vehicles to a cemetery. Not far from your location."

"Cemetery," Burke mumbled to himself. "Why a cemetery?"

"Not sure. But they stayed for quite a while. It looked as though they were searching for something among the gravestones."

"The flash drive," Burke said. "Did they find it?"

"I don't think so."

"How many men did he have with him? And how can you be sure?"

Lily went quiet.

"Lily," Burke urged. He had no time to waste. "You there?"

"I'm here. Not sure on the head count. But I'd say no fewer than ten. Probably closer to twenty."

"Damn, that's a lot."

"And Burke . . ."

"What is it?"

"From the looks of it, one of those men assassinated Lopez."

"What—you saw it happen—how?"

"Hacked into the security system at the cemetery. It was a little dark, but I still saw a man pull the trigger with my own eyes. It wasn't easy to watch, Burke."

"Are they still there?"

"Yes. But I don't know for how long. Looks like they're packing into their trucks and getting ready to leave."

"Okay, Lily, thanks. I gotta go."

"Wait, Burke."

"Yeah?"

"It sounds like the body count is starting to rise. Be careful. Please."

Burke *was* careful—most of the time. Until careful was no longer an option.

CHAPTER THIRTEEN

Jones and Sammy found an SUV parked outside with the keys still dangling from the ignition. It seemed that the men who attacked the building were in a hurry to get inside and finish the job. After loading Bear's limp body into the hatchback, Burke took the steering wheel and drove southwest. Mack was the passenger. They were excellent with directions—they had to be as SRs in the air force. The three others sat across the backseat.

"What's the word from Langley?" Jericho said.

"Rajabi was spotted at a nearby cemetery. And from the CCTV footage that Lily hacked into, she saw someone put a bullet into Lopez."

Mack cursed under his breath, then said, "Damn. They still there?"

Burke nodded, then took a corner in the SUV faster than he should've, causing the tires to squeal, but he didn't lose control.

"How many men are we talking about here?" Jericho said.

"Lily thought ten, maybe twenty."

"*Twenty*!" Jericho didn't mean to shout. With a lower voice, he said, "That's a helluva lot."

"It's nothing we can't handle," Mack said and eyed him in the backseat. "Right, Burke?"

Burke gave him a smirk and a nod, but deep down, with twenty enemies, they would likely encounter more casualties to their own team. Not a battle Burke would take lightly. Especially after the senior member of the group had been killed. Now all were looking to Burke for tactical decisions, not that he couldn't handle it—he'd overseen many missions in his career—but this one seemed . . . different somehow. They were going in blind, without much intelligence to go on. At the very least, it was ever-changing intelligence, with an adversary hell-bent on destruction against the West.

"There's Rajabi's men," Mack stated as they pulled up on the cemetery.

Burke quickly studied his surroundings. There weren't many trees in the area. No buildings to use for cover. From their position there was no good tactical maneuver for a successful mission with limited to no casualties.

Burke slowed the SUV.

"What are you doing?" Mack said.

"What's it look like, Mack? This is not the time and place to pick a fight. Not out in the open like this."

"What do you mean? They're right there. No more than a hundred yards away. We can take 'em."

"I agree with Burke. This wouldn't be a great tactical position," Sammy said.

"The mute speaks. Well, isn't that the damnedest thing," Mack said.

"Anyone ever call you an oxygen thief, Mack?" Sammy said.

Mack whipped around and shot him a stern gaze. Then his mouth turned up and he said, "So he does have a personality after all."

"You know I'm right, Mack," Burke said. "Look around. There's no place to take cover. What do you want to do, just drive up on them and have a shootout in the middle of a cemetery? Old West style?"

"Well, yeah."

Burke laughed. He knew his friend was always ready, if not looking, for a fight, but this was not the time nor the place.

"What's your plan then?" Jones spoke up from the backseat.

"You said it yourself, Jonesy. Before we left. The mission seemed to lack . . . planning, for lack of a better word. I say we wait here. See where they go. Follow the convoy and take them when the time is right. On our terms. Not Langley's."

"When will that be?" Jericho said.

"Hard to say. But I imagine Rajabi tried to check in with the men he sent to take us out. Or at the very least, he heard the explosion that went off. He's probably gonna check that out."

"Ever give any thought to the fact that we're driving in the very same SUV that his men arrived in?" Jones said.

Burke found his friend's eyes in the backseat. "Didn't think it would come to that, but now that you say it, yeah. Could be an issue if they catch sight of the SUV."

"I still think my way is better," Mack said. "We have the element of surprise on our side."

"If we had more time to surround the cemetery, I'd agree with you, Mack. But we don't. Most, if not all, are inside their vehicles and will be moving out shortly."

"What about the girl?" Jericho said. "If they already killed Lopez, I doubt she will be breathing much longer."

"As long as she hasn't given them the flash drive, she's safe."

"And if they take her back toward Damascus?" Sammy asked. "What then? We follow them into hostile territory?"

"Finally, some sense," Mack said. "I knew I could get on the mute's side."

"Yeah, I don't know, Burke, that sounds like we'd be taking a big risk," Jones said.

All had excellent points. But the matter remained: they were too exposed. And a standoff in their current position could be a death trap.

"The more we talk the more . . . ," Jericho said.

"More what?" Burke said.

"Well, I do have an alternative solution," Jericho said.

"What's that?"

"We still have a couple RPG rounds in the back with Bear."

"What?" Burke shot him a look. "We do?"

"Yeah. They were in the back, pushed up behind Bear," Jericho said. "And look, the men aren't in their vehicles anymore. Looks like they're scattering. Could be a way we get around them and flank them. Light 'em up with the RPG rounds. Take out their convoy. Kill Rajabi and rescue the girl."

"It all sounds good in theory," Burke said. "But still—"

"Still what?" Mack interrupted.

Burke turned to Jones. "What do you think, Jonesy?"

"I'm with Jericho. There are too many what-ifs if we let this go on any further into Syria. You know this place is crawling with rebels. ISIS. The Kurds in the north. Not to mention the government forces if they sniff us out. We can't take the risk of them getting away. Or losing the girl. Saving her *is* the mission, no matter what Stallone said in the briefing."

Burke let out a breath that he'd held in. He knew they were all right. Even though he didn't like the plan, a shootout was their only option. Maybe he was just second-guessing himself because of the unnecessary risks he'd put Jones and Mack in back in Nigeria. He wasn't losing his edge, but he definitely wanted to make fewer mistakes.

CHAPTER FOURTEEN

RAJABI OPENED HIS DOOR AND YELLED, "CYRUS! WHAT ARE WE waiting for? Let's move."

After slamming the car door shut, he turned back to Veronica. She leaned her head against the window and wept.

"There was never another copy, was there?" Rajabi would not let up. Not on her, a known CIA operative.

She shot a look his way, then yanked her bound hands toward him, but they were secured to the door, and she couldn't break free. Through tears, she said, "I'm never going to give you access to that building. Not now—not ever."

Rajabi gritted his teeth and reared his hand back, about to slap her for her insolence, but he never got the chance. Shots echoed in the night. Rajabi bent down and took cover behind the front seat of the car and watched out the windshield just as an orange glow of fire tore through the air. The RPG struck the SUV in front of the convoy and sent it sky high.

The power of the explosion shook the doors and glass of the vehicle. His eyes went wide, and he gripped the seat in front of him tightly.

He glanced over at Veronica, whose emotion of pain and sadness softened and turned to relief. She knew as well as he did that her government was coming to rescue her.

Rajabi turned to his right to see Cyrus running away from the vehicle and taking cover from another RPG. Rajabi shuddered again as he watched another vehicle burn. Then he looked back at the driver's console. The key fob was in the cup holder, exactly where Cyrus had left it. He couldn't wait to determine how many enemies had arrived or what their plans were. Rajabi jumped into the front seat and pressed the ignition button.

The engine sparked to life. He shifted the car into drive and slammed down on the gas pedal. The tires slid over the loose rock, but once they caught, he spun the steering wheel back into position and raced into the cemetery.

The SUV bounced up and down as he drove over the uneven ground—even knocked over a few headstones on his way past. He found it difficult to navigate the terrain, as his headlights continued to jump as he drove.

There was an opening ahead. The road wound its way in a semicircle and led out to the main roadway. That was it, his chance to put distance between himself and the threat. He had to get away from this danger; if the Americans caught up with him, he'd be without his loyal entourage. But it didn't matter. All that mattered was escaping alive and making sure he had Veronica in tow.

Once on the roadway, he glanced up at the rearview mirror. Someone was following him. He strained to recognize the vehicle. *Cyrus*, he thought. Wishful thinking. As he continued to drive, the car fired shots out the driver-side window.

Out of instinct, Rajabi ducked to avoid the shots, but they came fast and furious, and whoever was following him wasn't giving up easily.

Burke gripped tight to his rifle; his post was on the east edge of the cemetery, and he watched as Rajabi sped by. He felt helpless as he imagined Veronica terrified in the backseat. He might've had a shot at Rajabi, but he couldn't risk hitting her.

He witnessed Mack drive up from behind in hot pursuit in the very same SUV they had arrived in. After shooting off the RPG rounds, Mack must have jumped in to give chase.

Mack. What the—. Burke called out through the comms, "Jones, you seeing this?"

Jones offered no response. Why would he? He and the others were locked in a firefight, same as Burke.

Burke fired on a man, dropping him, then he ran north to follow Mack in the vehicle. Not that Burke would hope to catch him, but more to offer cover in case some of Rajabi's men were able to fire off a lucky shot as Mack gave chase.

"Get your head down," Rajabi yelled over his shoulder toward Veronica. "This idiot is going to get you killed."

More shots came, but they were nowhere close. Rajabi was beginning to think that the man pursuing them was either a horrible shot or somehow intending every bullet to come close but missing on purpose to scare him into slowing down.

The cemetery road was nearing its end. Up ahead was a ninety-degree fork. If Rajabi turned right, a large tree would make for a shield between him and his chaser. If he went left, the man in the SUV would easily cut him off.

Rajabi slowed slightly as he turned right. The tires squealed, and he momentarily lost control. The man from behind was ten feet off his bumper and closing fast. Rajabi pounded his foot on the gas pedal, but the vehicle didn't react how he wanted; instead, a belt slipped, and the car slowed as the RPMs revved. Rajabi looked over his shoulder and saw the man pulling up on the passenger side.

The man wouldn't dare ram him. No way he would risk hurting one of the CIA's assets. So Rajabi yanked on the steering wheel and slammed the SUV onto the shoulder.

There was a rock hidden in the darkness that Rajabi didn't see, neither did the man driving alongside him. It was a sharp boulder protruding from the ground. The second the man in the SUV hit that rock, the SUV ramped straight toward the sky. Rajabi did his best to watch in the rearview, but all he could see were the vehicle's lights breaking out as the SUV came crashing down on its passenger side.

Rajabi pulled away from the scene and laughed at the irony. He used the mirror to look at Veronica. "You see, your government has once again failed you. As long as I have you, they'll *never* find you."

CHAPTER FIFTEEN

"Mack," Burke called out through the comms as he witnessed the scene from the opposite side of the cemetery. "You there? Can you hear me?"

Mack didn't respond and Burke couldn't move. He was bogged down by enemy fire, and there was no way he could shoot his way out.

"Jonesy, Mack's down. The SUV overturned just outside the cemetery. Can you get to him?"

It took about five seconds for Jones to call back. "Negative, Burke. I'm on the southwest end and taking heavy fire."

Burke cursed under his breath. He watched through his scope as an enemy ran toward him through the labyrinth of headstones. He took aim and fired, dropping the man instantly.

Burke looked across the cemetery and watched a few men—maybe three—moving north toward Mack's crash site. He had to run and protect his friend. On the roadway that both Rajabi and Mack had just driven down, there was an opening with sparse trees and little cover. Not the best tactical decision, but what choice did he have? If he didn't, his friend would be surrounded and killed.

Burke sprinted across the road and came to a tall pine. Burke watched them slow down and spread out to surround the overturned vehicle.

Burke had to make a choice. He could stop—try to eliminate all three with precision shots from over a hundred yards—or keep running in the hope that Mack was able to shoot his own way out of the threat.

The men closed in on the SUV. They moved toward the back door. It was now or never. Burke dropped prone and steadied his rifle best he could. He took aim and fired a round. The man closest to the SUV dropped to the ground. The other two whipped around and began firing at Burke, but since he lay in the shadow of perfect darkness, their shots went high and wide. Burke fired again and dropped the second man. The third fled south and back into the heart of the cemetery.

This was the chance Burke was looking for. He pushed off the ground and sprinted toward the crash site. When he came close, he ducked under a tree and looked at the SUV as it lay on its side.

"Damn, Mack," he mumbled, then in a forced whisper said, "Mack, it's Burke. If you hear me, don't shoot. I repeat—hold your fire."

Burke heard a groan come from inside the SUV but couldn't make out any words. He reached the back door first and tried the handle. Locked. He moved to the driver-side door. Mack was there, still buckled in, but his head was dangling to the right.

"Mack, you alive?"

He tried the driver's handle, but it, too, was locked.

Mack lifted his head to see Burke standing outside the car, but Burke could tell he was woozy, as his eyes rolled around in their sockets trying to focus.

"Can you unlock the door?" Burke said.

Mack didn't move. As Burke was about to tell him to duck for cover so he could bust out the glass, the unmistakable scent of gasoline filled his nose.

Burke jumped toward the backseat window and broke it out. He jumped inside the SUV and reached for the seat belt that locked Mack in place.

"Sorry about this buddy, it might hurt a bit." Burke unlatched the buckle, and Mack was sent tumbling to the passenger seat floor.

Getting him out of the vehicle was going to be a chore. Because the vehicle was on its side, the door wasn't going to stay open. Mack was not a light man. And pulling two hundred pounds of dead weight out a broken window was no easy task, even for a man like Burke.

After pulling Mack into the backseat, Burke heard footsteps. He held his finger to his mouth and told Mack to keep quiet. Then he grabbed his sidearm from his thigh holster.

"Burke, Mack, you in there?" It was Sammy. Burke heard it through the comms and from outside the SUV.

"We are," Burke said. "I need help getting his giant butt out of here. And we need to move fast—I smell gasoline."

"Me too. I'm coming to the door now," Sammy said.

Once Sammy showed, Burke strained to stand Mack up. Burke pushed from under his arms, and when they had him standing, Sammy pulled him through the broken window and out of the vehicle completely.

Burke jumped through the opening and asked Sammy, "Is everyone dead?"

"Can't tell, but the bullets stopped flying a minute ago. We either got 'em all or they fled. Saw three or four men escape in a truck. Went south. No idea what happened after that."

"Good," Burke said.

"I'm going to get Bear out of the back."

Burke watched him move toward the hatch. "Be careful. Remember there's gasoline everywhere."

"Need any help?" Jericho said as he arrived at the crash site. Both Sammy and Jericho nodded to each other and headed to get their man. "We'll be back with Bear in a sec."

As Sammy and Jericho moved away, Mack regained some awareness. "Ugh, what happened?" He rubbed the back of his head.

"Looked like Rajabi ran you off the road," Burke said. "Couldn't quite tell from my position. I was too busy shooting the bad guys."

Mack tried to muster a laugh, but he soon winced in pain.

"Ouch. Don't make me laugh," Mack said. "My ribs hurt."

Burke looked him over. He had some lacerations and from the look of it maybe a mild concussion and some bruised ribs.

"Did you get him?" Mack said. "After he ran me off the road—did we get Rajabi?"

Burke shook his head no. "He got away."

"Damn," Mack said.

"But we lived to fight another day, Mack. And once he stops running, maybe this time we can put together a better plan for exfil for V."

"What makes you think this plan was fubar?" Mack laughed. "Ow, why do I do that to myself?"

As their laughter ceased, Jones walked up. "I counted ten dead."

Burke added, "Sammy said he saw a few get away."

"I saw the same," Jones agreed. "What about Rajabi?"

"Escaped with the girl," Burke said. "Went north to who knows where. But wherever he goes, we'll find him, and we will get her back. I swear to you, Jones."

Once everyone was accounted for, Burke and the others walked south to find another vehicle. It was time for them to rely on Lily's skill set. There was no way to track either vehicle that had escaped. And with one injured man and another dead, it was time to regroup.

Bear's body would need to be flown back to the United States and prepared for burial. And although Mack was tough, he needed a doctor.

Once they reached the south end of the cemetery, Sammy and Jericho split up to search for keys to one of the remaining vehicles while Jones went to search for Lopez's body. Burke lifted his satellite phone and called Lily.

"Burke," she shouted into the phone, frantic.

He had forgotten she had access to the cameras on-site and likely watched the entire firefight from the comfort of Langley.

"I'm fine, Lily."

"What about the others?"

"Bear's gone," Burke's head fell.

"I know. You told me already, remember?"

With all that had happened, Burke had forgotten. "Yeah, sorry.

Mack's hurt too, but he'll recover. Jones went to search for Lopez's body. But the worst news is, we lost Veronica. Rajabi still has her. And we have no idea where he took her."

"I'm on it, Burke. I'll see if I can find his vehicle and track him down."

"Some of his other men escaped, too, but they're likely to double back to wherever Rajabi lands. So, if you can't lock on to Rajabi, maybe find his men, because I guarantee they'll lead you to him."

"Roger that. What else do you need?"

"A place to rest up. Recover. And we need to find a way to get Bear's body out of here. Send him home. Lopez, too, when we find him."

Burke heard Lily typing on her end. As Burke listened, Jericho appeared from behind a truck and showed Burke a set of keys. "Got one, Burke."

Burke held up his finger and waited.

"Um . . . ," Lily started.

"Um, what?" Burke insisted.

"There's a classified black site close to your location, but I don't have the clearance to access its coordinates. That's going to take Stallone's approval."

"Well, then, go and wake the old man up."

"Burke, it's like six-thirty here. I mean, the guy's old, but I don't think he's in bed yet."

"It was a figure of . . . ," Burke said. "Can you just get him on the phone?"

"All right, all right, keep your pants on," Lily said.

Burke spoke off the phone to Jericho who waited with the keys in his hand. "Lily is finding a place for us to rest up until she finds Rajabi's location."

"Where?" Jericho said.

"Supposedly at some black site close by."

Jericho curled his lower lip. "Nice."

Someone came back on the phone, but it was not Lily's sweet sensitive tone. "*Burke*! What the hell happened?" Stallone barked.

"Rajabi is in the wind, sir."

"What? How is that possible?"

"Well, sir, he was in a vehicle and drove away." Burke matched Stallone's rude line of questioning with his own snide tone.

"I'm not in the mood for jokes, Burke. How did you let him get away?"

Burke ground his teeth. He wanted to reach through the phone and slap Stallone, but he kept his composure and told him the rest of the story.

"That still doesn't explain how you let him escape, but I see why you're in need of sanctuary. I'll have Lily send you the coordinates to the black site."

"We won't let Rajabi win, sir. Once we're able to refuel and get Bear and Lopez ready for transport back to the States, we'll track down Rajabi and rescue Veronica."

"How do you know she's even still alive?" Stallone said. "For all we know, she gave Rajabi the flash drive's location, and he dumped her dead body on the side of the road somewhere."

Burke sucked in a breath. He knew Stallone could be right, but he didn't want to believe him. "You're right, sir, that could have happened. But let's not speculate until we have proof. Lily will find Rajabi, and once she does, we'll track them down, rescue V, and find the flash drive."

"I hope you're right, Burke. If we can't get to Rajabi, that flash drive means everything."

"And getting V back."

"Of coursc," Stallone snapped again. "That goes without saying."

"I don't think it does, sir."

Burke expected to hear a response from Stallone, but he was gone, and Lily came back over the phone. "Burke, it's me," she said. "The base is called *Site 10-10*. It's near the Lebanon-Syria border. In the mountains. I'm sending you the coordinates now. After you've taken a rest and gotten Bear and Lopez out, let me know if you need anything else. I'll be working to find Rajabi on my end."

"Thanks, Lily."

"You're welcome, Burke."

Burke hung up, and Jericho said, "Where are we going?"

Burke showed him the phone and the coordinates.

"That's close. Like an hour northwest, but . . ." Jericho stalled and looked Burke in the eyes. "Isn't that rebel territory?"

Burke shrugged. He knew they didn't have much of a choice. Before they could load into the vehicle, Jones came running up from behind Burke. He stopped to catch his breath and stared into empty space.

"What is it, Jonesy?" Burke sensed something was off.

"Lopez is gone."

Burke looked over Jones's shoulder and back toward the cemetery. "What do you mean, gone?"

"His body . . . it's not here."

Burke dropped his head and muttered to himself. "Are you sure? Why would they take his dead body with them. That doesn't make any sense."

"You're right, Burke, it doesn't," Jones added.

"And you're sure you checked everywhere? The entire cemetery?"

"I did. All over. He's not here, Burke. He's gone."

CHAPTER SIXTEEN

RAJABI STEPPED INTO THE MORNING SUNSHINE. HE'D SPENT THE night at a safe house in southern Syria. It was not the time to return to his compound north of Damascus; he simply needed to avoid the American threat.

As he paced outside, he went over the previous night's events in his mind. Veronica refused to give up the location of the flash drive before passing out due to exhaustion. And he was at his wits' end with his attempts. It seemed she would rather go to an early grave before revealing her secrets. And in all honesty, he was fine if it had to come to that.

As he pondered his next move, his phone vibrated in his pocket. He answered, "Dimitri. How good of you to call." His tone was sarcastic. "You fled before we could reconnect. I figured you would be there to help me question the Americans. If I'm honest, since you were a no-show, I never expected to hear from you again."

"Sorry, Saam. I was pulled away due to the conflict. You know my face is easily recognizable." Dimitri spoke of the five-inch scar from his temple to his chin. "I couldn't risk being seen with you. Not by anyone in the village. Not with the rise in tension in Israel and the border. Plus, I didn't know if the Americans would eventually make it into Israel. You know you cannot afford to be seen having a Russian connection in that part of the world."

"So, what, you just decided to send me into the lions' den alone?"

"You asked for the location of the CIA operatives, and I delivered —you knew the risks."

"I suppose I did," Rajabi muttered.

"And after I sent you the text? How did that turn out? Finding the operatives? Did you use the information to get what you were looking for."

Rajabi huffed. "Yes, but it did not go according to plan. Some of my men were killed by a military operation in conjunction with the CIA. No doubt they came into Syria to rescue their operatives."

"So how did you get away?"

"I took the girl and drove my way out. Left Cyrus and the others behind."

"And you have the girl now?"

"I do." Rajabi stared over his shoulder at the building behind him. "She's still asleep. Or at least pretending to be."

"And is she going to give you the location of the flash drive?"

"That doesn't seem likely. No matter what I've done or threatened to do, she doesn't seem to change her mind. I can't seem to find her breaking point. Our only option was using the information on the other operative, Lopez. I threatened his family, and he caved. Gave us a lot, but that still didn't lead to the whereabouts of the flash drive. As much as I hate to say it." Rajabi looked back toward the house. "I think I need them both."

"Well, you know Iran is getting close to pushing the button on Israel. Getting close to a full-blown attack."

"Yes, I'm aware. And they know where I stand. They need me," Rajabi said. "That's why they are paying me so handsomely. They need deniability. Iran doesn't want to start a world war. And that's exactly what they'd be doing if they attacked Jerusalem. Especially if it turned nuclear."

"So why not just shoot the rockets off? Why not take your shot now? Why wait?"

"Iran is not giving me the greenlight until the flash drive is recovered. Again, they do not want their secrets out. And trust me, there's more on that drive than just the missile silo locations. We're talking names and addresses of government agents inside the United States, United Kingdom—"

"And why is that information on the flash drive?" Dimitri asked.

"I added them for protection. For myself. But ultimately, you know that I'm a businessman. Wars get expensive. And they don't last forever. So . . . when the time is right, I assume that information will be important to a lot of people in the world."

"You'd use it as blackmail?"

"Call it whatever you like. Ultimately, it's a way for me to be protected on all sides."

Dimitri went silent. After a few seconds of dead air, another call came in. When Rajabi stared at the screen, only the name, Cyrus, stared back.

"Dimitri, I'm getting another call, and I need to take it."

"I understand."

"Keep in contact with me. If you hear that Iran is making more moves to retaliate, you must warn me. I need to be kept in the loop."

"I will. And you do the same."

"Good-bye, Dimitri."

"Good-bye, Saam."

Just as Rajabi hung up the phone, he switched to the other call. "You survived the military onslaught, I see?"

"Almost not. No thanks to Americans," Cyrus said.

"How many of my men fell?"

"I don't know, sir."

"How many are with you now?"

"Two others. And the American."

"The American?" Rajabi's voice went up. "You still have him?"

"I do, sir. Picked him up when he regained consciousness in the cemetery and escaped."

"Cyrus, that's . . ." Rajabi wanted to thank his man, but he didn't know how to say it. "You did good."

"Thank you," Cyrus said. "Where are you now?"

Rajabi gave Cyrus the coordinates of the safe house.

"And what about the girl? Did she give you the location of the flash drive?" Cyrus said.

"No."

"She's not giving in?" Cyrus said.

"No. Won't utter a word no matter what I do."

Cyrus sighed. "I would've figured after we beat her and Lopez bloody, and she witnessed you fire a round toward Lopez's face, she would've rolled over and led you directly to the building."

"This is why you cannot let Lopez out of your sight," Rajabi said, worried. "I have no leverage on the woman. But Lopez, desperate to save his family, will tell me the location of the building where the flash drive is being hidden. We just have to figure out how to get into it. I just might have another solution to that, Cyrus."

"What's the solution, sir?"

"If we cannot get Veronica to cooperate, maybe we can use the other contact that Lopez spoke of. The women watching the live feed."

"But how will we use her, sir?"

"That remains to be seen. All I am saying is there are multiple ways to skin this cat, Cyrus. And trust me, I think this plan could work."

Rajabi hung up on Cyrus and made his way back inside the safe house. He walked over to Veronica who was asleep on the dirty floor. He watched her for a moment. "So . . ." He bent down into a squat and stared at her. "Your time may be running short after all. And if this works, my need for you will end. And then. . . so will your miserable life."

CHAPTER SEVENTEEN

Black Site 10-10 was located near Mount Hermon on the Syria-Lebanon border. Burke had never been to that part of the world, places he'd been reading about recently in his Bible. The words on the pages only lived in his imagination, but now being where Jesus walked made the words seem more real, more alive, than ever before.

As Burke closed his eyes and turned his face to the sun, he basked in the glow and warmth that beat down on him, and his mind wandered away from the Bible and the mission and turned to his wife. He smiled at the thought of her. Their last few months together had been great. Their relationship had blossomed and seemed to be hitting its stride. The deep, piercing sadness surrounding AJ's death had lessened. His depressive state had subsided. The wedge between them over their son's death, however unfair it had been, was gone. Burke could see the light at the end of the tunnel, and a reconciliation seemed all but a foregone conclusion.

Jones interrupted his pleasant reflection. "What's our next move, boss?"Jones interrupted his nice thoughts

His smile faded, and he started walking toward the infirmary where doctors were tending to Mack's wounds. "Have you seen Mack since we got here? How is he?"

"I have no idea." Jones walked with him.

"Let's see if he can continue. I need him. I need both of you with me. The SEALs are fine, but you and Mack have my back. I don't know how Jericho and Sammy will respond to my leadership now that Bear's dead."

"I'll stay on 'em," Jones said. "Keep 'em in line."

"Thanks, Jonesy. I knew I could count on you."

They rounded the corner of the first building before stopping outside the entrance of the infirmary. Jones grabbed hold of Burke's arm.

Burke stared down at his friend's tight grip. "What is it?"

Jones shook his head from side to side. "I just can't figure it, Burke."

"What?"

"Why we couldn't find Lopez's body. Of all the missions we've done together, have you ever seen that? Ever seen a group take an enemy's dead body in the middle of a firefight?"

"Never. Not once," Burke said. "But maybe . . ."

"Maybe what?" Jones said.

"Maybe Rajabi's plan is to . . . I don't know, parade his dead body on film. Put it on the internet. Send Lopez back to the CIA in pieces to scare us off. Who knows, the guy's a terrorist."

Jones stared at him for a moment. "That doesn't sit right, Burke."

"I figured. What's your theory, Jonesy? Clearly, you have a different perspective."

"What if he's alive? Somehow got out during the firefight. Maybe even got away from the cemetery somehow."

"I think we would've found him. Or at the very least, after the fight was over, he would've found us."

Jones shook his head. "Still, Burke, I just don't know."

Burke turned and walked through the doorway. Mack was sitting on a bed with his legs dangling over the edge. His shirt was off, and there was an icepack wrapped around his ribs on either side of his body. He also had gauze taped over the lacerations on his head and face.

"You look like you've been through hell," Burke said.

"Some might call it hell, I call it Tuesday," Mack replied.

They shared a laugh, which sent Mack into another wince in pain.

"Sorry, not sorry," Burke said as he and Jones walked over to meet Mack at his bedside.

"What's doc say?" Jones said.

"Said I have a mild concussion, some contusions on the ribs, and got four stitches here and three here." Mack pointed to his right temple and left cheek.

"So you gonna be ready to move out in a couple of hours?" Burke felt free to joke a bit now that they were with him and knew he would be okay.

"You know I am." Mack hopped off the table, but quickly reached back to stabilize himself and keep from falling backward.

"I wasn't serious, Mack. No way you're going with us. Not like this. You need to recover."

Mack stood tall to face Burke. "Why is it that I'm the one always getting hurt on these missions? You two idiots never seem to take the brunt of anything."

"That's because you're the reckless one," Jones said. "You act first and ask questions later. We're the calculating ones." Jones pointed back and forth to himself and Burke.

"Ha," Mack said, laughing. "You're calling Burke calculating? That's funny. I seem to remember, just a few months back, he jumped over a wall with over twenty armed men on the other side without giving any thought or, to use your word—calculation—to anything. Not to mention all the moronic things he's done over the past twenty years on countless other missions."

"Be that as it may, Mack, I think it's best you sit this one out . . . again." Burke winked.

Mack shook his head from side to side. "One of these days, I'm gonna finish a mission with you two."

"Or maybe you're getting too old for this," Jones said.

Mack reached for his friend and grabbed his head. "Them are fighting words." They playfully smacked and grabbed each other, until Burke broke up their little spat.

None of the men realized the doctor was standing inside the room and staring at their childish behavior.

"Ahem," she announced.

Each man shot to attention and stared back at her. She was a tall woman, almost six feet. She was long and lean but filled out her doctor's coat. She had olive skin and jet-black hair tied up into a high ponytail.

"I see your pain meds have already kicked in," she said.

"Not really, ma'am. This is just some playful banter. I don't need meds to take down the likes of him." He rolled his head at Jones.

"I see," she said as she started walking closer. She looked down at her feet and didn't see Jones and Mack still slapping each other in the foreground. "If you gentlemen will excuse us, I need to give Mr. Mack one more final exam before I give him my recommendations for recovery."

"Roger that, ma'am," Burke said.

He pulled at Jones's arm and led him out of the room. Once they reached the warmth of the sun, Burke heard the ringtone of his satellite phone.

"Who is it?" Jones asked as Burke lifted the phone from his pocket.

"It's Langley," he told Jones, then answered the call. "Lily, what do you got?"

"Not much, Burke. I was unable to track down Rajabi, but I was able to track the secondary vehicle. The one that traveled south out of the cemetery. You were right, Burke. It seems they made their way back to Rajabi. He's held up in some safe house in southern Syria."

"And what about V? Is she still alive?"

"I have no confirmation of that yet. All I have are satellite images. No CCTV. Nothing that can give me facial recognition at this time."

"Do we know if Rajabi has the flash drive?"

"Again. No confirmation of that."

"How do we know if the house they're staying at wasn't where V hid the flash drive in the first place?"

"We don't."

"So what *do* we know?"

"Like I said, not much."

Burke took the phone away from his ear and rolled his eyes.

"What?" Jones said.

Rather than answer Jones's question, Burke put the phone back to his ear. "Have you made contact with Emily?"

"Not yet. She should be landing at any moment. When she does, she's meeting with an asset who supposedly has more intel on Rajabi."

"Who is it?" Burke said.

"Her name is classified, and I don't want to say it over the phone, but she's with foreign intelligence."

"What does she have that can help us here?"

"I don't know, Burke, but for now I think we need to sit tight and wait to see what Emily finds out."

"You know, I don't like sitting on my hands, Lily."

"I know. You're a man of action."

Burke sighed, knowing there was nothing left to say. "Thanks for the update, kid."

"No problem, Boomer."

She hung up. Burke looked at his phone and wondered if he had said something wrong. No one had ever called him a boomer before, nor did he even know what it meant.

"What'd she say?" Jones said.

"She called me Boomer."

Jones laughed it off, and Burke said, "Looks like we're gonna be sitting tight for a while, waiting for Emily to get confirmation. Once she lands, she's supposed to be meeting with someone who has intel on Rajabi. Maybe his current whereabouts, I don't know. And neither did Lily, it seemed."

"That's not good, Burke."

"No, Jonesy. It most certainly is *not*."

CHAPTER EIGHTEEN

EMILY LAID HER HEAD AGAINST THE HEADREST OF THE AIRPLANE seat. She was sitting in row 19, seat A. Sure, she also had the window to lay her head against on the long flight over from Washington, but she didn't get much sleep due to the constant barrage of kicking between the two brats seated behind her. She wanted to reprimand them on multiple occasions. She even tried to get the attention of the absentee mother who sat beside them, but the mom was too busy watching movies or TV shows on her phone to parent their intolerable behavior.

Just as another kick came, Emily peered over the top of her chair and shot them a stern glare, then glanced at their mother. The boys mumbled under their breath in Arabic. Emily understood the language, but she couldn't quite hear exactly what they said about her. It wasn't until she reprimanded them in their native tongue that their heads went back against their own headrests, and both sat stick straight.

At her words, the mother of the two boys peered up from her cell phone and furrowed her brow, as if to say, *How dare you speak to my kids like that*. She told Emily to mind her own business and turn around.

Once Emily was facing forward again, the two children snickered, making fun of the strands of hair sticking out from under her hijab. Emily wore the head covering knowing she needed to do her best to fit in with the culture. Also to hide her identity and not draw unnecessary attention. This made the situation with the children behind her beyond irritating.

The pilot came over the speaker and said they would be starting their descent into Amman.

"Finally," Emily mumbled to herself.

The airport was south of the city of Amman, and the address Stallone gave her for V's contact, Natasha, was just north of the city. She would need to find a ride to Natasha's last-known residence.

"Why are you headed to Jordan?" the woman seated next to her asked.

Emily eyed her. "I'm a reporter."

"Oh, really? Do you have a story you're working on?"

"I do."

That was the perfect opportunity for Emily to rehearse her cover. She was curious to see how her lies would make the woman react.

"What's the story?"

"It's for a magazine actually," Emily said.

"Which one? I love magazines." The woman reached into her bag and pulled out three. They were beauty magazines. All ones you would find at an airport store.

Emily laughed. "None of those. I'm not much for beauty tips."

The woman shared a laugh as well.

"I actually write for *National Geographic.* We're breaking down new discoveries in Petra. Trying to nail down a timeline as to when the findings originated."

"That sounds . . . uh, interesting," the woman said, but Emily could tell she wasn't truly interested in the documentation of historical artifacts.

Emily winked. "Sure is."

The woman turned toward the aisle to grab the customs form from the passing flight attendant. She passed Emily a form and said, "I've been getting kicked the entire flight too. Some people's kids." She shook her head from side to side. "Just no respect."

Emily nodded in agreement, but she knew it was just as much the parents' fault as the kids.

Once off the plane, Emily waited in line at customs. The line wasn't long, but it was long enough for Emily to practice every what-if scenario in her mind. And the customs line in a foreign land is enough to make even the most seasoned covert agent sweat, from the questions the customs agent asks to the way you look—or the way they want you to look. If anything seems off to them, or maybe they just don't like the way you sound, or the story you tell them isn't believable enough, your mission could end before it even begins. And the rest of your life could change because of one small discrepancy in your story or timeline.

Emily looked to her left and noticed the woman who'd sat next to her on the plane. She was in the line beside her own, one person ahead. They shared a smile. Then the woman stepped forward, and she was next to her own customs counter. As the woman stepped forward, Emily witnessed the two brats and their mother approaching a different counter two lines away. She wondered how they got to the counter so fast. *Probably cut in line,* she thought.

Emily went back to staring straight ahead. There were two people in front of her, and then it was her turn. She breathed a sigh, and her heart rate climbed. Another person moved through the line, and she was on deck. She went over her cover story one last time in her head. As she looked to her right, she saw her friendly neighbor, which reminded her of the details she had pitched to the woman on the plane.

See. Just like I told the stranger. Emily Ryerson. A reporter for National Geographic. Here to document history.

As Emily was rehearsing her story in her head, she saw a flash of movement out of the corner of her eye. She saw the brats jumping up and down and pointing at her. She scrunched her brow. Why were they pointing? Then her stomach sank when she noticed the mother was speaking to the customs agent and pointing directly at Emily.

Emily spun around. They couldn't have been talking about her. She searched the area for another culprit. Maybe someone they knew. But there was no one. Only her. She continued to stare, and soon the customs agent called over to a security guard standing along the wall near the exit.

Emily shifted her gaze and dropped her eyes to the ground and swallowed hard. Her heart rate climbed above 150 and had no signs of slowing. But even though her insides churned, she had to keep it together.

"Next," the customs agent called in broken English in front of her. Emily didn't hear him right away, so he spoke louder. "Next, please."

The person behind Emily tapped her shoulder. She looked around and saw that the other customer was hinting for her to move forward. Emily turned and saw the vacant spot. She stepped toward the agent and held out her paperwork. She was still glancing over at the woman and her two kids, who never took their eyes off her.

"What is your business in Jordan?" the customs agent said.

Emily peered over him to see the security and agent still talking. Sweat bore into her hairline, but thankfully it was covered by the hijab she wore.

"Do you speak English?" he said. Then he asked the same in Arabic.

Emily nodded. "English is fine. Yeah, sorry, here you go." She handed over her passport and other papers.

The man looked at her photo and repeated, "What is your business here?"

"I'm a journalist. Here to document artifacts in Petra."

The man eyed her and nodded. What she said sounded reasonable to him. "How long is your stay?"

"One week."

The man coursed through her paperwork for a few seconds. "That's what your visa says. Do not make your stay any longer. Do you understand me?" He stamped the passport and held out her papers to give back to her.

She nodded, and as she stepped forward, the security guard two rows away, still staring her down, started walking toward her.

Everything inside her told her to run. Get away as fast as possible. But she knew she couldn't do that. Only guilty people run. And she was far from guilty. At least in that instance. The only thing she may have been responsible for was putting two brats in their place and telling a mother how to parent.

Emily remained calm and still and shut her eyes. She held them closed for longer than a normal blink and waited for what was to come.

Nothing came. When Emily opened her eyes, the security guard had already passed by and moved on. Maybe he was called off somewhere else. Perhaps an emergency.

She breathed a huge sigh of relief and moved out of the terminal toward the ground transportation area of the airport. She needed a ride. She found the taxi service area and looked toward the board to see the set taxi fares based on distance. She didn't know how far the address was away from the airport, but she did know the address was north.

She stepped up to the corner and told the man where she was headed. He handed her a ticket and guided her to the curb where the first available taxi would drive her to her destination.

A car pulled up. It didn't look like the typical yellow cab she was accustomed to seeing in the United States or in movies; instead, the car was a black Mercedes with tinted windows. She held tight to her belongings as the driver dipped out of the front seat and came to open her door to the backseat.

"Welcome to Amman," the man said as he held the door open.

She nodded and stepped inside. The interior was black leather, and the temperature was a perfect seventy-two degrees. Not too cold and not too hot.

"Water?" the driver asked as he looked at her in the rearview, holding a bottle.

She shook her head. "No, thank you."

"Very well." He reached for his seat belt and buckled the strap across his chest. "We should be at your destination in less than an hour."

An hour? Emily didn't think it was that far, but she nodded and stared out the window.

Nerves fluttered in her belly, because she was at the mercy of a random Jordanian cab driver. He seemed friendly enough, but Emily had met all kinds of men in her past. And one can never tell who the evil ones are until it's too late.

CHAPTER NINETEEN

THE CAB DRIVER WAS RIGHT. THE DRIVE FROM THE AIRPORT TO the address took about an hour. Emily reached forward and handed him a tip, even though she'd already paid a flat fee at the airport stand. As she stuck out her hand with a ten-dollar bill, the man locked her hand in his and stared into the rearview directly into her eyes.

"Be careful when you step outside this car. You never know who you can trust. With the current war happening in Israel right now, terror groups are looking for any reason to pick up a traveling Westerner. Especially a Western woman traveling alone."

Emily's heart stopped. As she stared back at him, she thought of her training with Naomi. "Money is always the great equalizer," Naomi would say. "Especially in foreign lands."

"Tell you what," Emily said. "Why don't I give you a few more dollars, and you forget you ever saw my face or where you dropped me?"

The man nodded up and down slowly, then let go of her hand.

She reached into her bag, took out two twenties, and handed them over. "How's this for foreign relations?"

"I have no idea what you're talking about. In fact, I don't see anyone in my cab right now. Must've disappeared into thin air." He grinned, and Emily dropped the cash on the front seat and got out.

She stood on the sidewalk in front of a large building—maybe a hotel, she wasn't sure. Every building in the city looked the same: off-white rectangular box, four or five stories, with little grass and no trees outside. It was a verifiable concrete jungle.

Emily walked through the automatic doors into the lobby. The color scheme inside wasn't much different. Nothing but stark white walls set against drab colors on the furniture. The only pop of paint was the fire-engine red on the front desk area walls.

A woman was sitting behind the desk. As Emily neared the counter, she was reminded of what the cab driver said. She did not want to give away her American accent, so in perfect Arabic, she relayed the address.

The woman behind the counter stood up, then started writing on a piece of paper. Emily couldn't tell what she was writing, not until the woman flipped the paper around. It was only one word, and it was misspelled and scribbled.

Mone.

Emily dropped her head to the side but didn't linger long in her annoyance. All she had to go on was the address Stallone had given her, but she didn't know how much money the woman expected. Too much and she wouldn't last the day. Too little and the woman might clam up and keep her mouth shut.

She took out the smallest bill she had—a twenty—and pushed it across the countertop. The woman picked up her head and grinned but remained silent. After picking up the bill, she disappeared into the back.

Uh, hello, Emily thought as she tossed her arms to the side and scrunched her brow. Her stomach fell because she figured she'd insulted the woman. About ten seconds later, the woman reappeared. She smiled and in broken English said, "Follow me."

There was no elevator, so the woman led her to the end of the hallway. She opened the door to the staircase and started climbing. They didn't stop until they reached the third floor. Once through the doorway, Emily peered down the long hall.

As they walked, Emily took in her surroundings. The hallway was narrow, and the carpet had the same bright red hue as the border surrounding the lobby countertop. The walls were caramel brown, and the doors were bright white. The woman stopped halfway down the hall, turned around, and looked Emily square in the eye.

"This one," she said, again in broken English. Then she reached into her pocket and lifted a key. She reached for Emily's hand, opened it, and placed the key inside.

"Uh . . . ," Emily started. She wanted to say more but held her tongue. As the woman walked away, she couldn't believe what twenty US dollars had bought her. "Not much for security," she mumbled to herself.

She looked at the door. It was within arms' reach. But now Emily was at an impasse. Should she just put the key in the lock and walk in, or would it be smarter to knock first? And was that room even the right room? For all she knew, the woman from the front desk had led her into a trap, right into the arms of the very men she was trying to avoid.

She stepped forward and put her ear to the door. She heard some rustling. Someone was inside, moving around fast, maybe trying to hide something. She lifted her ear away and pushed back. She raised her hand and moved the key toward the lock, but stopped when she heard a suspicious noise. She couldn't quite tell what it was, but it sounded like someone racking the slide on a pistol.

If someone was behind the door with a gun trained on her, they would likely shoot first and ask questions later.

Emily's heart was in her throat. Her next move would very likely change the trajectory of her entire life.

"Natasha," she whispered and waited. She said her name once more, this time louder.

The door swung open, and the woman behind the door grabbed Emily by the back of the head and pulled her into the room, throwing her to floor. Emily bounced up quick as a flash and was ready to fight like Burke had taught her. However, the other woman was also fast, too fast for Emily, and she already had her Glock pointed at her face.

"Relax . . . easy . . ." Emily kept her eyes low and tried to downplay the situation.

The woman snapped back. "Who are you? And why are you here?"

"A friend sent me."

"Friend? I don't think so. Not unless that *friend* wished you harm and a short life span."

Emily found the strength to look her in the eye and said the only thing she thought that might save her life—the truth. "I'm here because of Veronica Alberts."

Instantly the woman lowered her gun. "V?"

Emily nodded.

"What? Why? Is she dead?" the woman said.

"I was hoping you could answer that for me."

"I can't. Not right now at least."

"What do you mean?"

Apparently, she wasn't going to give Emily any more information.

"Sorry," Emily said. "How rude. I'm Emily."

"Wait, Emily? You mean, went-to-Duke Emily?"

"That's right. Me and V played soccer at Duke together."

The woman finally let go of the breath she'd been holding in and forced a smile. "Nice to meet you. I'm Natasha."

The woman took a seat on the bed.

"So she told you about me?" Emily said.

Natasha nodded. "She did. Said I could trust you if we ever met, but I . . ."

"You what?" Emily said.

"I have to say, honestly, I never thought we would get that chance."

Emily laughed to herself. "Well, that goes for both of us. I didn't even know V was CIA. Thought she was still a journalist with the *Times*."

The woman found that funny. "No. She's, uh, well, let's just say she left that world behind a long time ago."

Emily's eyes found the ground as she reminisced a moment about their soccer days at Duke and their past working relationship. "Me too," she mumbled.

"So, you have no idea where V is right now?" Natasha said.

"At this moment, no. But there was a mission just sent out to rescue her and Lopez. Six men. Dropped in from the sky last night." Emily trailed off.

"Rescue them? Did Rajabi track them down?"

"I don't know for sure. That's what the rescue mission intended to find out, but . . ."

"But what?"

"I was supposed to get a call once I landed that the mission was a success, but I haven't heard anything."

"And you have no way of communicating with the team?"

"I do, but . . . I wanted to talk with you first."

"Why?"

"Because the man leading the mission is someone I trust with my life."

"Famous last words of anyone who's about to be betrayed."

"Burke's not like that. He'd never. He literally saved my life more than once. And had my back on numerous other occasions."

"Okay, so where is this *Burke* guy now?"

"The mission was in southern Syria. That's where intel had V and Lopez tracked."

"That makes sense. The last communication I had with V was right before they left Damascus."

"And why were you in communication with her from here? Were you working together on something?"

She nodded. Then rolled her head, suggesting Emily follow her into another room. Once through the doorway, Emily was stopped in her tracks. On the TV screen there were four cameras set up looking at all the access points on a half-constructed building.

"What's that?" Emily said.

"That's where V has the flash drive hidden."

Emily's eyes went wide. "And where is it?"

"No idea."

"What do you mean?"

"I mean, I don't have any idea where that building is. All I have is the live footage, and if anyone goes inside without V's approval or if it's not V herself, she told me to detonate it. Things rigged to blow with thirty pounds of C4."

"Wait, what? Seriously?" Emily said.

"C4 is not something to joke about." Natasha smiled.

Emily choked on her next words; she didn't want to speak them into existence, but she had to, "What if she never comes back? Or you get word she's been killed?"

"Same result. She told me, if I get word that she's dead, I'm to blow the building and everything in it."

Emily tongued her cheek and said, "Well then, I think it's best we get ourselves some answers, don't you?"

"Couldn't have said it better myself. I'm sick of playing spy in this nightmare of an apartment. I just want this mission finished so I can head home to my warm bed and cats."

"Cats? Really? Wouldn't have pegged you as a cat lover."

"You know nothing about me." Natasha smiled.

"That's true, I guess. It's just, I assumed from your file."

"The CIA has a file on me?"

"Didn't your organization have a file on V?"

She grinned and said, "Yes. A thick one at that."

CHAPTER TWENTY

Burke was resting comfortably on a makeshift bed made from two-by-fours and plywood with only a two-inch mattress—not exactly the Ritz Carlton. But Burke found ways to sleep almost anywhere—if he was tired enough. He was having a dream. A nice dream at that. Not the nightmare he had been so accustomed to having—the one about losing his son in a drowning accident. That dream had somewhat faded over the last couple months.

He had come to grips with the reality that AJ's death was not his fault. Demons tried hard to convince him otherwise and keep him lost in the dark. And the dark is where the gross things grow. But now that Burke had found his faith and brought that fear into the light, he had less of of a tendency to fall back into the trap the devil seemed to ensnare him in.

A loud knock on the door shook him out of his dream. Burke stared up at the ceiling not knowing if the knock was inside his dream or if someone was standing outside his bedroom door. Another knock came. "Burke. You awake?" Jones said.

Burke rolled over and ambled toward the door. When he opened it, he rubbed his eyes and stared sleepy-eyed at his friend.

"Sorry, boss. It's Stallone." Jones pointed over his shoulder.

Burke slipped a shirt over his bare chest and followed his friend out the door. Jones led Burke to a conference room. Jericho and Sammy were both there. And to Burke's surprise, so was the director, Avery Stallone.

His eyes went wide at the sight of him. "Sir. How did you—?" Burke looked down at his watch, wondering how long he had been asleep.

"The *how* is not important, Burke. But the *why* is?"

"All right, sir. *Why* are you here?"

"To see this through."

Burke scrunched his brow. Sure, Naomi had accompanied him on some of his missions, but never her superiors. Never the boss.

"From this moment forward, I want you to consider me your handler."

Burke turned his head to the side. He was a bit shocked. Sure, they lost Naomi, but Burke expected Stallone to give them someone else from the agency, not take on his team himself.

Burke found Jones's eyes. They shared a concerned look, and both knew exactly what the other was thinking. Neither liked being interfered with, especially not in the middle of a mission.

Burke wanted clarification. "So, what's that mean exactly?"

"It means that I will be giving you strict instruction based on Lily's findings."

"Hey, Burke," her voice echoed from behind.

He shot around and saw her gripping her laptop under her arm and wearing a smile.

Burke smiled back. "It's good to see you, Lily." Then he whipped back around to face Stallone and started to speak but stopped.

"I can tell something else is on your mind, Burke," Stallone said. "What is it?"

"I still don't understand why you are here, sir."

"Because the director of national intelligence told me to come. He has the authority to make that ask. I admit, I was a bit thrown by the inquiry myself, but he insisted. Said he wasn't sure if you could pull off the mission. And then he said, and I quote, 'Especially in the light of one dead US senator.'"

Burke's heart sank. He had no idea that the director of national intelligence would be clued in to what happened a few months prior with the death of Senator Nicolas Wainwright. Burke and Jones shared a concerned look, but they couldn't say anything. Not in front of Jericho or Sammy.

"And with Bear already dead. And another on your team injured, well, I didn't put up much of a fight. I figured you could use the extra help."

As much as Burke wanted to tell him off, Burke knew Stallone was right. Having extra help couldn't hurt, especially help from inside the country.

"Fine, but you two stay here. At this site. No way I'm bringing you or Lily into the field. Not in the middle of a war zone," Burke said. "I'm not risking your lives for this."

"I couldn't agree with you more, Burke," Stallone said. "And I have another QRF team on standby if we need reinforcements."

Burke shook his head. "Unnecessary. I'm happy with my guys." He looked at each of his men.

"Your team was nearly cut in half on day one, Burke. I imagine the fighting will only intensify the closer we get to finding Rajabi. And if you're forced to go deeper into Syria. Lebanon, Iran, or wherever we track him, the mission will only become that much more difficult."

"Exactly the reason I don't want more men. With four, we can travel light and fast. In one vehicle. The last thing I want is a convoy of military men. We won't even get close to Rajabi if his allies see us coming. And I guarantee he has already had the dead men from the cemetery replaced."

"Fine. Then they will stay put for now. But if I sense that you're in over your head, Burke, I'm sending them out. Do you understand me?"

"Yes, sir."

"Good," Stallone said as he turned away from Burke. "Lily, show him what you found."

"With pleasure." She moved around Burke and opened her laptop. After quickly plugging in a cord, an image appeared on the screen. "This is the footage I found after tracking Rajabi's men. They drove from the cemetery and to this house in Syria. Watch what happens."

Lily hit the space bar and let the video play. It was an overhead projection from a satellite image she had recorded. Three men exited a parked car and walked toward a house, where they met another man. They were talking for what seemed to be a few seconds before one man disappeared into the house and in less than thirty seconds appeared with a woman in tow. The man in the image was grasping her head, then tossed her onto the ground. Lily was quick to press the space bar again to get the video to stop.

Burke found Lily's eyes, then Stallone's. He pointed to the screen and said, "Now we have video confirmation that Veronica is still alive."

Lily pressed the space bar once more.

Two of the men kicked dust in her face as she lay in the dirt, and another bent down to her level and tried to reach for her. Of course, they couldn't see the man's face or determine what he said, but then the man tried to help her up and she ripped her hand away. From the looks of the image, Veronica attempted to lurch and go after the man who'd bent down to her level, clearly enraged to see him.

At last, they picked her up and tossed her into the back of their vehicle, and that's when the video stopped.

"Where'd they take her?" Jones said.

Lily looked at Stallone. She didn't want to say anything until he gave the okay.

"They headed north toward Damascus," Stallone said.

Jones dropped his head, and Burke bit his lip.

"Like I said, Burke, this is not going to be an easy mission," Stallone said.

"Easy?" Burke said. "Maybe not. But we're the best you got."

Each man shared his own version of agreement.

Then Burke looked Stallone square in the eyes. "And V's last hope."

CHAPTER TWENTY-ONE

Burke was loading his gear and packing his magazines full of ammo when he received a call on his satellite phone. He knew it had to be Emily. He was quick to pick it up and say hello.

"Burke, is that you?"

"Yeah, Emily, how are you? Did you contact V's asset in Jordan?"

"Yeah, I'm with her now. But what happened with your mission? Did you find Lopez or V?"

Burke told Emily to hold while he walked past Jones, Jericho, and Sammy. All of them were doing the same thing as Burke—getting ready to move out by checking and double-checking their gear. Burke nodded at Jones and moved out of the ammo room for more privacy in case Emily asked a question he didn't want to answer in front of the others.

Once outside the room, Burke gave Emily the rundown of what had happened.

"So where is she now?" Emily said.

"Traveling north toward Damascus. We're not exactly sure where they'll land. Lily is tracking them as we speak, and we're supposed to be moving out within the hour."

"Can you keep in contact with me during your travels? I want to know everything you know. That way, we can confirm on our end."

"How do you mean?" Burke curled his lower lip.

"I mean, I'm looking at a live camera feed."

"A live camera feed to what exactly?"

"A building."

"What building?"

Emily paused for a moment. "A video feed with four cameras set up around the perimeter."

"Okay, but what's that got to do with this mission specifically?" Burke said.

"The live feed is set up for Veronica's asset in Jordan to monitor from a safe distance. It's where the flash drive is being hidden."

"*What*?! Are you sure about that?"

"That's what V's asset tells me."

"So why doesn't she just get us the address and we can bust down the doors, snatch the flash drive, and wrap this mission before anyone else gets hurt?"

"Because she doesn't know where it is.'

Burke scrunched his brow in confusion. "What do you mean?"

"I mean, she has no idea where the building is. Could be anywhere in the city. All she has are the instructions V left for her."

"What instructions?"

"The building's rigged to blow with C4. If Veronica doesn't show up alone to collect the flash drive, she directed her asset to blow the building with all inside. V took this mission very seriously, and apparently, she didn't trust many people with the secret. Which is why even her own asset has only video footage and no other information."

"Does she know when V was supposed to be there?"

"No. Only that V and Lopez were going to talk to her shortly after they departed Damascus, but she never received the call that they were on their way to the building to collect the flash drive."

"Has she heard from Lopez at all?"

"Don't know. Let me ask."

Lily showed up from around the corner. She saw Burke on the phone and didn't want to interrupt his conversation, so she bowed her head and waited. But Burke held the phone away from his ear and said, "What's up?"

"Rajabi returned to his residence north of Damascus," Lily said. "The place looks like a fortress, Burke. Stallone wants to go over a brief in five minutes."

Burke nodded to Lily and told her he understood. When Emily came back on the phone, she told Burke that Lopez did not get back in touch with Natasha.

"Do you know where he is?" Emily said.

"We do not. Lily couldn't find him on the cameras at the cemetery or fleeing the scene during the gunfight. It's weird. It's like he up and vanished into thin air."

"That is weird," Emily said.

"Look, Emily, we need to get briefed on the next mission, so I gotta go. But keep in touch with what you're doing, you hear me?"

"I do, Burke. And be careful."

"Same to you. And just because you're in Jordan doesn't mean you're in any less danger. Watch your back, and remember your training, you got me?"

"Got it. Talk soon."

Burke reentered the room and let the others on his team know that they were to be briefed. He followed them out, then walked back toward the same room he'd met Stallone and Lily in when they first arrived on their surprise visit.

Once they arrived, Burke was shocked to see others in the room. Two men in military fatigues, one standing at attention and the other in a chair.

"Who's this?" Burke said.

"This is your QRF team," Stallone said. "Well, the commanding officers anyhow."

"I thought we talked about this," Burke snapped.

It wasn't Stallone who responded but the man in the chair. His name was Severino Christiansen. Christiansen filled out the chair quite well. He was broad across the chest and shoulders and every bit of six foot four. He put off the consummate military lifer vibe and seemed as though he had seen a few things in his career.

"Avery and I discussed it. He gave me your side of the story, but I don't know if I see eye to eye," Christiansen said.

"How do you mean, sir?" Burke said.

"Well, since we know that Rajabi is holed up in his fortress north of Damascus, you're going to need more than four men to take him down. He's no doubt resupplied his losses at the cemetery and perhaps doubled down on security now that he knows we're in country. Going over his walls with only four men would end with all your families receiving folded flags. I'm not sure that's what you want. And I can guarantee you, that's not what the US government wants. This mission needs to be flawless—I mean, locked down with a clamp. No mistakes this time. Rajabi needs to be neutralized and the flash drive recovered."

"What about the girl?" Jones said.

"Again, that goes without saying," Stallone said.

"Does it, sir?" Burke said.

"What do you mean?" Christiansen asked.

"I mean that without the girl, we don't have the flash drive," Burke said and then filled them in on his conversation with Emily.

"All the more reason to add the extra men." Christiansen was adamant, and Burke knew he was right.

"So when do we head out?" Jericho said.

"Chopper leaves here at zero one thirty," Christiansen said.

Burke's shoulders fell. More waiting around. He hated it. He wanted to be in the action and loved the adrenaline rush that came with it, but the action would once again have to wait.

CHAPTER TWENTY-TWO

RAJABI CUT INTO A THICK STEAK. THE RED JUICES POURED FROM THE meat of the medium-rare filet and soaked the plate beneath the asparagus and garlic mashed potatoes. As he put the bite of steak in his mouth, Lopez stared at him from across the table. Rajabi hadn't spoken many words to him on the short drive north from the safe house. Rajabi felt the need to wait to discuss business until after he was in the confines of his own home.

"I expect you have come up with a plan to save your family," Rajabi said before he shoved another piece of steak into his mouth.

"Someone is . . . is still watching the location of the flash drive and if—"

Rajabi slammed the table with his open hand and cut Lopez off. He pointed his steak knife at him. "I'm not looking for excuses. I know someone's watching. The question is, what are you going to do about it?" Rajabi was testing the waters, trying to see what Lopez would do.

Lopez trembled. "I'm not trying to make excuses . . . I swear to you."

"Well, that's exactly what it sounded like to me."

Lopez swallowed hard and continued. "What I was saying is that someone is watching the location of the flash drive—"

"And it is rigged to blow up. That much you told me before," Rajabi said, cutting him off once more. "The question is, how are you going to go get it for me?" Rajabi pointed the knife toward the door. "It's not like we can use the girl. She'll never give us the location. It's up to you now. What can you do?"

Lopez floundered to offer a solution. "I can reach out to Natasha."

"And who is Natasha?" Rajabi said.

"The one watching the live feed. The one with her finger on the detonator."

"And what will you do when you make contact with her?" His question was somewhat rhetorical.

"I don't know, but maybe I could convince her that I need access."

Rajabi sat tall and leaned back against his chair and took in Lopez's story. It was unfolding exactly how he had planned in his own mind when he spoke to Cyrus after they had escaped the cemetery. "So your plan is to convince this . . . this Natasha woman to give you access?" Rajabi questioned. "I thought you and Veronica were supposed to enter together."

"We are. But as you said, she's not cooperating. I am."

Rajabi knew he had him. He knew Lopez would do whatever it took to save his family.

Then Rajabi continued. "Convince her that Veronica sent you by yourself—sent only you to retrieve the flash drive? Then in turn make sure she doesn't blow the building as you enter it?"

"Yes." Lopez nodded.

Rajabi reached for the napkin he had placed inside his shirt and tore it out. Then he wiped his mouth and called Cyrus over, who was standing guard by the door. Cyrus bent down and Rajabi leaned backward to whisper in his ear, "Get my phone."

Cyrus nodded and handed Rajabi a phone from his pocket, and while Cyrus remained close, Rajabi said, "Keep a close eye on him after this. If for one second you think he's trying to trick us, take him out."

Cyrus nodded and walked back toward the door.

Rajabi stared across the table; then he slid his phone across the wood. When the phone came to rest, Lopez stared at it in front of him. "What are you waiting for?" Rajabi said. "Get in contact with Natasha and execute the plan exactly as you said."

Lopez reached to grab the phone, but before he dialed, Rajabi said, "On second thought, come. Sit here. Next to me. You can make the call and put it on speaker so I can hear."

Lopez froze. He glanced toward the chair but didn't move at first. Then he stood from the other side of the table and walked over to take the seat next to Rajabi. After pulling his chair close, he glanced down at the screen but paused before dialing the number.

"What are you waiting for?" Rajabi said.

Lopez stared at solid wood and said, "The right words. Natasha is foreign intelligence. She's not some uneducated simpleton. If I say the wrong thing or give her any indication V is not speaking through my mouth, then you might as well kiss your flash drive good-bye."

"Then by all means, choose your words carefully," Rajabi said.

Lopez raised his head and closed his eyes and breathed in deep. "Think, think. What would V say?" he questioned out loud.

After another moment, he dialed the number.

"Hello," Natasha said.

"Natasha."

"Lopez? Is that you?"

"It is." His voice was frantic. "I'm . . . I'm—"

Rajabi was shocked at how good of an actor he was.

"Where are you?" Natasha interrupted.

Emotion rose, and a tear gathered in Lopez's eye. "I got away from Rajabi at the cemetery." He sniffled.

"It's okay. Calm down. I heard they couldn't locate your body after the firefight," Natasha said.

Lopez's eyes went wide in panic, and the tears disappeared just as fast as they came. Rajabi stared at him and went rigid.

"How did you know that?" Lopez asked weakly.

"We've been in contact with Langley. They had eyes on you through CCTV at the cemetery. Said you were shot, but then somehow got away in the firefight. No one knew where or how, but they couldn't recover your body after the shoot-out."

Lopez's chest rose and fell. His breath was short and rapid, as if under duress. "That's because I escaped. I can't explain it myself. I thought I was a goner." Lopez was trained by the CIA and adept at lying. He could concoct a story out of thin air. "I don't even know how I'm still alive . . . I guess someone's looking out for me, you know?"

"Where are you now? Are you still close to the cemetery? We have people in country. They can pick you up."

"No. I'm deeper into Syria."

"What? Why?"

"I was able to steal a car." He figured this would make his story more believable and earn him points for his bravery. "I followed the men who took V. I'm near their hideout now, but there's no way of getting inside to get her back. There are too many men guarding it."

"So what's your plan then?" Natasha said.

"To get the flash drive back. I know V told you we needed to be together to collect it, but . . ."

"Yes, she did."

"Well, that's why I'm calling. I'm letting you know that she wanted me to be the one to pick it up if she was unable. I need to get it as far away from Rajabi as possible and back in the hands of our government before they can—"

"Before they can what, Lopez?"

He exhaled deeply and then said, "Can extract it from her. By whatever means of torture necessary."

Natasha took a deep breath, trying to digest his story. "I . . . I . . . don't know, Lopez. V gave me specific instructions."

"V's *captured, Natasha*." It was the first time Lopez had gotten angry. He was thinking of his family and what Rajabi would do to them if Natasha didn't believe him.

Natasha went silent again, and Rajabi leaned back and rolled his eyes at Lopez's lack of tact.

Lopez's tone turned softer. "Natasha, are you there?"

"I am."

"So, what do you say? Do I have a green light to go inside? To get the drive back to the CIA?"

Again, she remained silent until he pushed again for her response.

"Natasha?"

She came back on and said, "Under one condition."

Lopez was taken aback. "What's that?"

"I meet you there. If we do this, then we do it together. It's the only way I'll allow you access."

Lopez found Rajabi's eyes. Rajabi nodded in agreement.

"That's fine with me," Lopez said.

"Good. Tell me where and when to meet you," Natasha said.

Lopez looked at Rajabi and spoke into the phone. "The building is in Damascus. I don't feel comfortable giving you the *exact* location of the building until we are both in the city. Just like you, I have to make sure we can trust each other."

"I understand," Natasha said.

"How soon can you get to Damascus?"

"I can be there in three hours."

"Then I will talk to you in three hours."

"See you soon," Natasha said.

"And, Natasha," Lopez said.

"Yeah?"

"Be careful when you're driving. We have a lot of enemies between Amman and Damascus."

"Don't worry about me. I'll find my way."

"Well, then yes, I'll see you soon."

After hanging up, Rajabi kept his eyes on Lopez, who shifted in his seat; Rajabi could tell he made him feel uncomfortable. "The flash drive is in Damascus?" Rajabi asked.

Lopez's head fell. He nodded, and before he could utter another word, Rajabi slapped him across the face. Cyrus immediately took steps toward them, but Rajabi called off his dog knowing Lopez would not retaliate. Lopez rubbed the side of his face and could hardly look up.

"Hold out your hand," Rajabi said.

Lopez held them on his lap.

"Hold out your hand," Rajabi repeated himself.

Lopez shook his head no. "No. We had a deal. You promised—"

"I promised I wouldn't kill your family in exchange for information about the flash drive. I never said that all your limbs would be spared for your insolence. Now hold out your hand, or I'll take them both off."

Lopez lifted his left hand and placed it on the table just as Cyrus moved in from behind Lopez and held him tight to the chair so he could not sneak away.

Rajabi grabbed ahold of his hand and placed his steak knife atop Lopez's pinky finger. "This is for all the pain and suffering you've caused me," he said. "Go ahead and scream, 'cause, no matter how loud you are, no one's coming here to save you." Then he pushed down on the knife, cutting off Lopez's finger.

CHAPTER TWENTY-THREE

NATASHA MOVED QUICKLY INSIDE THE APARTMENT, GRABBING LOOSE clothes and stuffing them into an empty duffel bag. Emily followed her every move, asking multiple times if she could help, but every time Natasha responded, "No, I'm fine."

When Natasha came to the bathroom, she looked every which way, frantically trying to figure out what to pack. It wasn't until Emily grabbed her by the shoulders and spun her around that she shook the anxiety away.

"What's wrong with you? Why are you so flustered?" Emily said.

Natasha's eyes found the floor. "It's V."

Emily empathized with her situation. She and V were close, too, and it's never easy losing a friend, especially a friend you trust. And in truth, so few in the spy world can be trusted.

Tears formed in Natasha's eyes as she looked back up. "I never thought it would come to this."

"Tell me about Lopez." Emily figured changing the subject would help to calm her nerves.

"Gilberto?"

"Yeah, what's he like? Did V trust him?"

"Well, yeah, I guess." Natasha shrugged.

"You guess? What's that mean?"

"I mean, from what I gathered, they've worked together on the Rajabi mission for a while. Sure, he has some quirks and has said some stupid things during their time together, but nothing that V considered dangerous. Why do you ask?"

"I don't know, it's not really what I'm asking, but more so, what Burke was asking. I could tell he was confused by Lopez's—" Emily stopped to use finger quotes. "Death."

"What do you mean?"

"I don't know. We can ask Burke more about it when we talk to him next, but my question to you is, do you think V trusted Lopez with her life?"

"I mean, yeah, I think so, but . . ."

"But what?" Emily pressed. "What is it?"

Natasha broke free from Emily's hold and walked into the bedroom to gather her thoughts. Emily followed close behind but stayed quiet while Natasha ruminated on her memory of V's exact words.

Natasha whipped around and said, "Okay. V didn't spell it out specifically to me, but she kept on repeating that she needed to be at the building with Lopez to obtain the flash drive."

"Okay. So . . . ," Emily started, "I'm guessing she didn't plan on getting captured."

"So . . . at the time she told me, I didn't really read too much into it. Honestly, it was right before she and Lopez went off to Damascus to get more intel on Rajabi and the flash drive. Then all hell broke loose. They always did their missions together. It was part of their legend—their cover. Sure, they were allegedly journalists, but they were also supposed to be a married couple. When she mentioned that she needed to enter the building, well, I thought maybe it was because they'd always be with each other. I don't know." Natasha threw her hands up. Like she was talking herself into a circle.

Emily sat on the nearby bed, put her hands to her face, and took in the story. "Do you think Lopez could be hiding something?"

Natasha shrugged and said, "I honestly don't know."

"Either way, we're gonna need backup. We can't go into this alone.

We can't meet him in the middle of Syria by ourselves. If he did turn, we'd be walking into a trap and be as good as dead."

"What are you thinking?"

Emily took out her phone. "I'm calling Burke."

"But I thought he said they were taking down Rajabi's compound tonight."

"I'm sure that *was* his mission. No doubt detailed by Stallone himself."

"And you think he'll, what, just defy that order and come over the border to help us?"

"I think that's exactly what he'll do."

"Why?" Natasha scrunched her brow.

"Because I'll ask him."

Natasha smirked. "What is it? You two dating or something?"

"Ew, gross. No."

"Then what?"

"Let's just say, he's like my big brother."

Emily held the phone to her ear, and on the first ring, Burke picked up. "Didn't think I'd be hearing your voice this soon."

"What? You didn't miss me?"

Burke laughed. "Like I miss visits to the proctologist."

"Funny, Burke."

"I thought so."

"What are you doing?"

"Watching Jones play *Call of Duty*. It's riveting over here. I'm just sitting on my hands, waiting for the greenlight to go take down some bad guys."

"What if I had intel that would suggest you get off the video games and move into Damascus right now."

Burke's voice went up in excitement. "You got me interested. What kind of intel?"

"Lopez is *alive*, Burke."

"What? Are you serious? How do you know that?"

"He just called V's asset in Amman."

"Why would he do that?"

"Because he needed to ask for permission to go inside the building that's rigged with C4. The one they were supposed to enter together."

"That's a strange ask."

"That's what we thought too. If he's on his own, why didn't he call Stallone?"

"Maybe he thought he needed to have access to the flash drive first," Emily said. "Maybe he didn't want Stallone to get excited over nothing." Emily explained the rest of the conversation between Natasha and Lopez.

"So you're heading there now?" Burke said.

"Not yet. Still pulling our stuff together. But we need you for backup, Burke."

"Nah, you don't," Burke said immediately. "You got this. Just remember what I taught you, and you'll be fine."

Emily held her breath. She couldn't believe her ears. Was Burke really going to sit this one out?

Then laughter came through the speaker. "I'm just kidding. Of course you need me. You always need me. And trust me, you can't do this alone."

She breathed a sigh of relief. "What about the other mission? What about Stallone?"

"Let me worry about Stallone. We'll be there. You can count on it."

"Thanks, Burke. I knew I could count on you."

"You always can, Emily. You always can."

Emily hung up the phone and stared at Natasha. "He's in."

Natasha smiled. "I guess he is protective over you, isn't he?"

Emily gave a sideways grin. "I told you we can trust him. And he's the best at what he does."

"I hope so. Because if Lopez has gotten into bed with terrorists, we're going to need all the help we can get."

"Well, then hopefully Burke can be our guardian angel."

CHAPTER TWENTY-FOUR

Burke stood up from the couch from where he'd been watching Jones. "Go find Jericho and Sammy. Fill them in on what Emily told us. Tell them we're moving out within the hour."

"You sure about that, Burke?" Jones said. "Need I remind you what happened last time you defied a direct order?"

Burke didn't need the constant reminder of what happened in Nigeria, but the question did need to be asked. Because Stallone would not hold back his anger once he discovered they were gone.

"Relax. If all goes according to plan, we'll be back here before he even knows we left. It will help our cause if we have the flash drive in our hands. Then we can do the mission with Christiansen and rescue V at zero one thirty."

"I suppose you're right," Jones said.

"I know I'm right. Now go."

Burke watched Jones leave the room. That sent Burke on a mission of his own. He may have needed to keep Stallone in the dark about their secret mission, but he had to clue in Lily. Because, well, they needed her help. They needed overwatch. They needed her to hack into a satellite and make sure they weren't walking into a trap.

Burke searched the compound for her. The first place he looked was the makeshift conference room where he'd met Stallone and Christiansen. She wasn't there. Then he walked through the door leading outside. The eight-foot walls in the open rectangular area led to a series of three doors. Burke walked through the area and saw Christiansen at the end of the corridor. He was talking with someone Burke didn't recognize. He kept his head down, not that he cared if Christiansen saw him; he just didn't want to be questioned.

Burke steadied his pace and walked past the two men without being seen. Burke pushed through the first door he came to, a restroom with only a single toilet.

"Do you mind?" a soldier said as he looked up and saw Burke.

"My bad."

Burke disappeared and ducked his head through the next door. There she stood, looking in the mirror and fixing her hair. Once she saw Burke, she shot up straight and fixed her shirt. "Burke, what are you doing? Why are you in here?"

"Sorry," Burke said. "These doors aren't labeled Men and Women. Didn't realize you were inside. But I do need to have a word. I'll wait outside."

A few seconds passed, and she came out of the restroom.

"What is it?" She stepped in front of him and had a worried look on her face.

Burke searched the area and made sure no one was around to hear their conversation. Christiansen had left with the man he was talking to, and no one else was there.

Burke leaned close and whispered, "I need to know, can I count on you?"

"What do you mean?" she said.

"I mean, if I ask you for help with something that no one else is to know about, are you in or out?"

"What are you asking? 'Cause if you're asking if I'm in or out on a chance for adventure with you, the answer will always be emphatically yes."

"That's what I hoped to hear."

She laughed and cracked her knuckles as if she was ready to dig in at that very moment. "What's the adventure?"

"We're leaving now. Me and Jones. He went to recruit Jericho and Sammy, and I'm sure they'll be joining us once they hear the mission."

"What is the mission?"

"We're going to get the flash drive."

Lily lowered her brow. "I'm confused. What about the mission to rescue V?"

"I feel like the two are connected, but we're not waiting until zero one thirty. We're going in now."

"Now? Like right now?"

"Yeah, we have intelligence. Something Emily concocted with the asset in Amman. They're meeting Lopez in Damascus."

"Wait, Lopez is *alive*?"

"Shh." Burke gestured by pumping his hand downward, letting her know to keep her voice down. "He is. And he made plans to meet up with Natasha to recover the flash drive."

"But I thought V had to be with him."

"Trust me, they've got a plan."

"Well, then yeah, I'm in. Tell me what you need me to do?"

"I need you to be our eyes in the sky. I can't stress this enough, Lily, this must remain a secret."

"Say no more." She flipped her hand.

"Great. Understand, though, however hard it will be to get this done, the harder part will be keeping it from Stallone. Once he figures out that we're gone, he's gonna search for answers. And he'll come looking for you."

"So why don't I just go with you? You know I can do all this remotely."

"No. Can't happen. I need you here. Safe."

"Safe, like 'hacking security cameras from a diner in rural Virginia' safe?"

"That was different, Lily."

"Was it? I mean, I seem to remember saving you and Jones more than a few times that night."

Burke breathed hard. She was right, she had. And if she hadn't detonated those bombs in the woods, who knows, Burke, Jones, and

Burke's wife could've joined Naomi in death the night they killed the senator.

"Look, kid—"

"Ugh." She threw her hands at her side. "I'm not a kid."

To Burke she was, but he knew she didn't like the label. "Sorry, Lily, this just isn't a fight you want to step in the ring for. Stay here. Help us from your laptop. There are more ways than one to be the hero in this story. You don't need to be the one pulling the trigger or the one getting shot at."

Her head fell. "That's not what I'm looking for." She kicked the dirty ground. "It's just so boring here."

Burke understood her frustration. He never liked waiting around either. He needed action. He craved the shot of adrenaline through his veins that made him feel alive.

"I get it, Lily. Just do this for me." He grabbed her chin and lifted it so he could look her in the eyes. "Please."

She nodded and smiled. "Fine. But you owe me, Burke."

"Whatever you want." Burke broke away. "I'll take you out for ice cream when we get back. Maybe a round of mini golf."

She turned her head to the side and rolled her eyes.

"You're the best. Keep your phone on." Burke pointed to her pocket and then jogged to meet up with Jones.

Burke found Jones, Jericho, and Sammy waiting in his bedroom. "Figured this would be the best place to chat."

"Agreed."

"So what's this I hear about Lopez?" Jericho said.

"He's apparently alive and kicking," Burke said.

"And what? Don't you think Rajabi might be using him as his errand boy?" Jericho said.

"That's one theory," Burke said.

"What's another?" Sammy cut in.

"That he's telling the truth and got away during the firefight. Either way it's a win for us. Emily and Natasha need us to back them up if their plan goes to hell. So, are you in, or are you out?"

Both men sarcastically looked shocked, then laughed, raised their rifles, and Jericho said, "We started this mission with the six of us. There are four now."

"Good math," Jones said with sarcasm.

Burke laughed.

"I say we go finish what we started," Jericho said. "Christiansen can take his mission and shove it."

"What about Stallone?" Sammy said.

Burke found Jones's eyes. "He won't say a word if we return with the flash drive. Not a word."

"And if we don't?" Sammy said.

"That's why I'm asking you boys if you're in." Burke's tone had turned serious. "Because coming back without the flash drive is not an option."

CHAPTER TWENTY-FIVE

Natasha led Emily to the parking garage. After putting their gear in the backseat, both women dipped into the front of the small white sedan. When Emily reached for the seat belt, it was caught and wouldn't budge. She looked at Natasha.

"It's broken," Natasha said matter-of-factly.

Emily's eyes went wide.

"Mine is too." Natasha grinned. "Don't be alarmed, I'm a great driver."

"I'm not worried about your driving skills." Emily fell hard against her seat back. "It's the other drivers we need to be concerned about."

"Relax, people here don't drive crazy."

"Sure they don't." Emily's eyes went up. "It's only one of the most populated cities in the entire Middle East. That's like saying people in New York don't drive crazy."

They shared a laugh. Natasha backed out of the parking spot and drove out of the garage. Once they turned onto the street, Emily couldn't believe the amount of traffic. The road system looked like a close-up picture of the anatomy of the human body, with veins and arteries traveling every which way in multiple directions.

"This place is a maze. How do you know your way out of here?" Emily stared out the window.

"I've been here for *quite* a while. You get used to it," Natasha said.

"I don't know that I could ever get used to this."

When they came to a stop, Emily peered over at Natasha, who was not taking her eyes off the rearview mirror.

Emily could tell something was bothering her. "What is it?"

"I don't know," Natasha said. "But I think someone may be following us."

Emily clenched her jaw. Everything inside her wanted to look over her shoulder, but she resisted and turned to stare straight ahead out the windshield.

"How can you tell?" Emily said out of the side of her mouth.

"There's a black SUV. Two cars back. It has been on us since we left the garage."

Emily gave in to temptation and glanced at the side mirror to see if she could see the vehicle Natasha described. But her vision was blocked by the oversize white-panel truck parked alongside the road.

"Can you lose him?" Emily said.

The light changed, and Natasha proceeded forward.

"Hold that thought. Let's just make sure I'm not being paranoid."

Natasha took the next right, giving Emily a clear view of the SUV following them around the corner.

Natasha glanced at Emily and said, "Yep. They're definitely following us."

"Any idea who it is?"

Natasha shook her head. "No telling. But . . ."

"But what?" Emily said.

"How did you get to my apartment?"

"What do you mean?"

"You obviously didn't rent a car, so how did you get there?"

"I hired a cab at the airport."

Natasha bit her lower lip and sighed. "The driver gave you up. Or maybe the woman at the front desk told a local gang about a Western woman who was traveling alone and was an easy mark. Or maybe the men inside the SUV are tied to a larger terror organization that caught on to me. Whatever the case, they're on us now."

"So, what do we do?" Emily said.

"Well, we have some options."

"Which are?"

"There's no way we can make it to the border. Once we get outside the city, they'll run us off the road or just open fire on us. And I imagine we'll be outmanned and outgunned."

"That's a hard pass," Emily said. "What's the next option?"

"Try to outrun them." Natasha rolled her head toward the SUV behind them. "Here. Through the city."

"In this thing?" Emily looked around the car. "With no seat belts?"

"Don't be fooled. You can't judge a book by its cover. She's got more in here than you think."

"Is there a third option?"

"Not that I can think of," Natasha said.

For the first time, Emily peered over her shoulder and saw that the SUV was gaining ground. And she knew that their best bet to stay alive was to drive, and drive fast. Try to lose the SUV in the maze that was Amman, Jordan.

Emily looked over at Natasha. "Floor it!"

Natasha followed the instruction, and she pounded her foot down on the pedal. The tires screeched and smoked as they cut someone off who was crossing the road in front of a McDonald's.

Emily watched the black SUV speed up to follow them.

"They're coming," Emily said.

But Natasha didn't bother responding. She stayed focused. The last thing they could afford was to hit a pedestrian or get in an accident that would render their vehicle useless.

The road turned to the north. Natasha followed it at a speed higher than the posted limit. And as they traveled, the highway came into view. It was above them, like a typical overpass you would see in the States. The road turned right to parallel the highway, and as they proceeded to the next intersection, Natasha had a choice: veer left to catch the on-ramp of the highway, or take the ninety-degree right turn down a one-way street.

"They're gaining on us," Emily said, continuing to watch the SUV. "Go faster."

Instead, Natasha did the opposite; she began slowing down.

"What are you doing? They're gonna ram us."

Suddenly, Natasha yanked up on the emergency brake and ripped the wheel to her right to take the right turn at a high speed. The car fishtailed slightly. The SUV spun to its right as well, but soon lost ground to the much smaller and agile sedan. Natasha pounded her foot down on the gas pedal again, and they sped down the one-way street.

The next roadway approached, and it came to a T. They could turn right and make a circle, or they could go left. The decision was easy; the only move was left, but just as Natasha made the turn, the SUV caught up from behind and rammed their bumper, causing the car to spin. The man in the passenger seat opened fire and sent bullets flying through the windshield of Natasha's car. None hit their mark.

People on the sidewalks screamed and ran in terror. The gunfire was not something they were used to seeing or hearing, especially in broad daylight. This wasn't a war zone. Amman was a civilized city, with civilized people.

Natasha's car faced the wrong direction, which meant she had to drive in reverse. At least until she was able to get her vehicle free from the bumper of the SUV. Natasha draped her arm across the seat and stared over her shoulder so she could see where she was going.

After the car was put into a spin, Emily's go bag was at her feet. She reached down and grabbed the Glock that Natasha had given her at the apartment. Emily lifted it out but couldn't yet return fire because there were too many innocent men, woman, and children nearby. She did not want to risk their lives with a wayward shot. The only way she was going to use the Glock was if she had no other choice or knew exactly where the bullet would end up.

There was a large enough opening just behind them.

"Hold on!" Natasha shouted. Then she yanked the wheel and spun further in order to straighten out the car's direction.

More bullets came, this time shattering the back windshield. Both women ducked out of instinct, but again the bullets flew wayward.

"That's twice they missed. I don't know that we're lucky enough for them to miss a third time," Emily said.

Natasha stared in the rearview again. The SUV was hot on their tail. She didn't need to say it, but Emily knew it to be true. They weren't going to escape. They needed a new plan.

"There's a store up ahead here on the left. I'm gonna stop there, and once I do, I need you to get out and sprint inside and don't stop running. There's a back door in the store that leads to an alleyway that leads to another building. Go inside, get to the staircase, then run all the way to the top. Hide out on the roof."

"What? No." Emily didn't agree with the plan. "I can't. Not without you."

"Take the Glock. Only use it if you have to. The noise alone will bring on authorities or unwanted visitors."

"No. I don't like this plan. We need to stay in the car. If we get out, we're as good as dead. We can use the car as a weapon. Like the agency taught us."

"They have automatic weapons, Emily. No car can take on automatic weapons." Natasha was speaking the truth. "Listen to my words. Do what I say. I'll find a way to get to you."

"What if you can't?"

"I will. Now, *go*!"

Natasha pulled to the side of the road. Emily jumped out before the car came to a full stop, and Natasha sped away.

Emily sprinted across the road and into the electronics store, but she was not alone; one man had jumped out of the SUV and was after her, gaining ground with every step he took.

CHAPTER TWENTY-SIX

EMILY BURST OPEN THE GLASS DOOR AND SPRINTED INTO THE middle of the store. The man behind the counter yelled at her in Arabic for scaring his customers, but she had no time to offer an apology. On her way to the back door, she dodged two patrons waiting at the counter to purchase their items. The man chasing her was not so lucky, as one of the patrons stepped in his path, but he tossed the patron to the ground. This allowed Emily the separation time she needed to reach the back door on her own.

Once outside, Emily saw two alleyways, not just the one Natasha had mentioned. One alleyway split right and led back toward the street, and the other split left and led to the staircase Natasha had instructed Emily to take.

Without considering her options, Emily simply reacted and turned left. As Emily reached the staircase, the man threw open the back door of the electronics store. Emily glanced over her shoulder and saw him notice her. She was still in plain sight.

She bounded up the staircase as fast as her legs would allow. She noticed there were only three stories to the top. If only she could get to the top and find something to hide behind . . .

The man cursed at her in Arabic from below, yelling insults, apparently trying to bully her into stopping. Rather than making her scared, it only made her move faster. When she reached the rooftop, she took less than a second to survey her options. There were four oversize AC units spread out, so she moved to the closest one and hid behind it.

She leaned close and listened, then closed her eyes for a moment to calm her breathing. This was a tactic Burke taught her during their training together. And she would need to rely on that training. She reminded herself of his words. "It's not being the strongest physically that matters. You have to be mentally tough. Sometimes you need to depend on your brains and your resolve to win the fight."

She heard the man's steps getting closer. She gripped the handle of her Glock. She was ready to use it, but she knew it should be her absolute last resort. He was close, within ten feet to her right. As he crept closer, Emily moved toward the left side of the AC unit to use it as a shield. Then she heard him occupy the space she had just vacated. He let out a sigh after seeing she wasn't there.

Emily could've just as easily stood up and shot the man dead, but again, she wanted to use her brains. Sure, she was an okay shot, but it takes a lot of nine-millimeter ammo to bring down a man in a rage if it's not placed in the right part of his body.

Emily circled around to the front of the unit as she heard the man continue pacing toward her. Instead of following her trail, however, he turned off and moved on to the next AC unit, about thirty feet from her current position. It was likely his back was turned to her, so she lifted her head slightly above the unit to see if she could capture a good look at him as he walked away.

For the first time, Emily was able to witness the man's size—wide across the shoulders, maybe outweighing her by some seventy-five pounds. A battle of brawn with a man like him would not turn out in Emily's favor, but she knew deep down she was ready to fight if it came to it.

The man checked the right side first, then moved onto the back. Once he was there Emily ducked out of sight, in case he decided to look back to where he came from. But he did not. The man continued on to the next unit. It was diagonal from her position across the rooftop.

Emily moved to the corner of her AC unit. She watched the man move on to the next unit as she used the side of her own as cover. When the man got close, Emily noticed something on the ground beneath him, but the man didn't seem to notice it. It looked like a piece of metal, but it was hard for Emily to tell exactly what it was.

As the man stepped away from the shard on the ground and worked his way toward the opposite end of the AC unit near him, Emily concocted a plan. Soon the man would be closest to the edge of the rooftop, and Emily could make her move.

When the man's back was turned, Emily scurried across the rooftop and somehow leaned against the unit closest to him without him seeing her. Emily looked down at the shard, and sure enough, it was a one-by two-foot piece of metal set with jagged rolled edges.

She tucked her Glock in her belt line as she reached down and picked up the metal shard. She gripped it tight. Emily took a deep breath and prayed silently to herself. When she felt the man was in the best position, close to the rooftop's edge, she made her move. She jumped out of her crouch, and just as the man's eyes went wide, Emily chucked the piece of metal like a Frisbee. The metal struck him in the chest, but that's not the part that Emily planned to use as the weapon. The metal shard was just the distraction she needed. Emily lowered her shoulder and put it into the man's stomach, sending him off-balance. His arms floundered for something to grab onto but caught only air.

His momentum carried him back to the two-foot concrete edge of the rooftop. Emily felt a sense of relief, as it was only a matter of seconds before he would fall and gravity would take over. But she didn't expect the two-foot concrete barrier to catch the man's weight, enabling the man to stabilize himself.

He laughed halfheartedly and said in broken English, "Now you die."

Emily had no interest in dying. She pulled the Glock from her waistline and squeezed the trigger. Since she was only a few feet away, each bullet hit its mark. On the seventh burst, the man tumbled over the edge of the rooftop and fell three stories to the waiting concrete.

Emily lowered her weapon. She didn't dare walk to the edge to look. She knew the man was dead, but now it was only a matter of time before the local authorities heard the shot. After all, they were probably only a few blocks away investigating the car chase she had been in earlier.

She needed to get out of here, and fast, but she was alone without a car. And where was Natasha?

CHAPTER TWENTY-SEVEN

After climbing down the staircase from the rooftop, Emily heard the unmistakable sound of a siren. The sound echoed in the area between the two buildings and was getting louder and louder. She paused and stared down the long alleyway leading out to the street. People were running along the sidewalk toward the front of the electronics store.

After ducking under a clothesline, Emily continued to walk toward the commotion. She needed to blend in with the masses in order to get to a safe place and put distance between herself and the crime scene. But where that would be, she didn't know. She was in a foreign land with her asset in the wind and no way of getting ahold of her.

More and more people congregated on the sidewalk, and just as the sirens arrived at the scene, Emily reached the building's edge. Knowing that she couldn't turn right, in fear of running into the store owner or the patrons inside the store who could identify her, she turned in the opposite direction and walked against the current of the crowd.

Many people bumped into her on the small sidewalk and spoke in their native tongue. "Someone jumped off the building," they said. "I heard gunshots," another said. Emily continued walking. She wanted to put as much distance between herself and the dead man as possible. The last thing she needed right now was to get caught.

Another police cruiser sped down the street, coming in the direction she was walking. She felt out of place: if the officer saw her walking away from the scene of the accident, it would be like a spotlight from heaven shining down on her.

Without giving it another thought, she turned and followed the crowd. The crowd in front of her stepped into a light jog, but she kept her pace. She walked slowly and kept her head down until the police car passed. As she rounded the edge of the building, some of the people stepped into the street to get a better view of the body. Almost every person had their phone out and was filming the dead man on the road.

Their behavior was off-putting, and as Emily looked around, she couldn't help but judge them for their lack of humanity. Shaking her head at them, she was about to turn her back to the scene when she saw the store owner in the street talking with one of the officers. Before Emily could turn around, the store owner caught sight of her. His eyes went wide, and he stood on tiptoe, as if to make sure his eyes weren't deceiving him.

Emily whipped a 180 and started walking away.

"Hey, *wait*!" the man screamed.

She quickened her pace. Not into a sprint, in case the police weren't following; she didn't want to attract attention.

She glanced back and saw someone pushing through the crowd trying to lock on to her location.

Screw it, Emily thought and jumped into a sprint. As she approached the corner of the next building, Emily heard a loud whistle from across the street. Emily shot her focus toward the sound. It was Natasha. She was inside the driver's seat of a different car, not the same white sedan they'd left the apartment in.

Emily sprinted into traffic, narrowly avoiding a passing car. The sound of the car horn turned all attention to her as she ran toward Natasha. The store owner chasing her stopped running once he saw her recklessness.

"There, there!" he called out and pointed.

Emily gave one last glance back toward the scene before dipping into Natasha's car.

Once inside, Natasha said, "Are you okay?"

"I am now, thanks to you."

Natasha slammed the car into gear and peeled out of the parking space she'd occupied.

"What happened?" Natasha said as she drove.

Emily told her everything, then said, "I didn't have a choice. I had to shoot him."

Natasha checked her rearview and side mirrors for any sign of the police, but so far no one was anywhere in sight. "Sounds like you had no other way out."

Emily nodded. "How did you get away? And where did you find this car?"

"Stole it. I stashed the other car once I put the SUV in the ditch."

"Say what? How'd you ditch the SUV?"

"Rammed him into an embankment not too far from the electronics store."

"Nice. I may have underestimated you."

"No." Natasha grinned. "You underestimated my car."

Emily found her comment amusing. "I did and I'm sorry. Won't happen again."

"Would've kept her, too, but she had too much heat on her. This car is clean, and if we can lose the police in the city, then . . . we should be able to reach the border."

"That's a big *if*," Emily said. "No way they didn't see us leave back there."

"I'm sure with all they have going on, chasing down a random girl they can't connect to anything isn't high up on their priority list. Crime in this city is taken very seriously, and the police don't just go hunting down bad guys and squaring off like the cowboy movies from the US. It's a process."

"Well, I guess that works in our favor then, doesn't it?"

"Definitely," Natasha said.

"I'm not worried about the police finding us at this point. I'm more concerned about the group who tried to abduct us in the first place."

"What do you mean?"

"There might be another car. Someone else following us."

Emily glanced out the window to look for anyone following them. "How will we know?" she said.

"Odds are, there won't be, but we need to be aware. And once we're out of the city, we should be—what's that American expression? —free home."

Emily eyed Natasha, then understood what she was trying to say. "You mean, home free."

"Yeah, that one." Emily smiled, but then Natasha spoke again.

"At least until we reach the border of Syria. Then, well, then we might encounter a whole host of other problems."

"Like what kind of problems?"

"Depends on who's working the border. By the way, how much money do you have?" Natasha said.

"A little less than two hundred."

Natasha sighed. "I just hope that's enough."

"Enough for what?" Emily said.

"For the bribe we'll likely have to pay."

Emily's face turned sour knowing a little over a hundred US dollars wasn't exactly a lot of money.

CHAPTER TWENTY-EIGHT

Burke stared out the window of the SUV they stole from the black site. He watched as the landscape turned from green hills to vast sand and desert. Traveling on that specific stretch of road during the day was dangerous—very dangerous. Syria was hostile toward any Westerner, and he just hoped, for their sake, they did not run into an opposing force before they were able to scout the building.

"Burke, you bring any more of those drones?" Jericho asked.

"Sure did. Brought two, in fact."

"Oh, nice. Can I fly one?" Jericho said.

"Sorry. Only Air Force Airmen allowed." He grinned and smacked Jones in the shoulder as he drove. "Can't have the navy going and destroying our precious gear."

"Whatever, man," Jericho said. "I'm sure anyone with half a brain could fly one."

"That's exactly why you can't." Burke peered over his shoulder and smirked.

"Ha-ha, very funny," Jericho said.

"What? You said it, I didn't," Burke said as his phone vibrated. It was Emily. He put it on speaker so everyone could hear her update. "Emily. What's up?"

"*Burke*!"

He could hear panic in her voice. "Yeah, Emily, I'm here. Are you okay?"

"For now."

"What is it—what happened?" She caught Burke up on the latest events. He was proud of her bravery. "Sounds like our training has paid off then, huh?" Burke figured making light of the situation might put her more at ease.

"It did, but now we likely have more problems."

"What kind of problems? Are you at the border?"

"Yes. We made it out of the city, and we're coming up to the border now."

"So, what's the problem?"

"Looks like there's some kind of checkpoint. You know, like the one we saw in Nigeria after President Kazah was killed."

Of course Burke remembered. It was hard to forget. "Which part? Do you think you might have to blow through the checkpoint like we did? 'Cause if that's what you're suggesting, I would highly recommend you do not take that path."

There was a moment of silence on the other end. Burke scooted to the front of his seat and leaned his hand on the dashboard as he waited.

"Emily? You there?" Burke pulled the phone off his ear to make sure he was still connected.

"I'm here, Burke, it's just . . ."

"Just what?"

"I don't know what questions we'll face with the added security at the border."

Burke knew exactly what to say. "Just go over your cover. Tell them what they want to hear. I'm sure Natasha has been through it before. Just rely on her."

"She has. But she said she's never seen the extra security checkpoint before. They must be looking for something—or someone."

Jericho leaned in from the backseat and spoke loud enough for Emily to hear. "Do you have extra blankets, pillows, clothes? Anything accessible or within arm's reach?"

"We do, but what's that have to do with anything?" Emily said.

"Stuff them into your belly. Make it look like you're pregnant. Tell the men at the checkpoint and the gate that you're going over the border to see your family. You're trying to get back to your husband before the baby comes." Burke gave Jericho a weird look. Then Jericho said only to him, "It'll work, trust me, but they gotta sell it."

"Emily, do what he says," Burke insisted.

"I'm already on it. We're the next car in line."

Burke could hear shuffling on the other end; then it was silent and the phone went dead. He looked down and knew she was gone.

He turned toward Jericho. "How do you know that will work?"

"Saw it in a movie once."

"What?" Burke scrunched his brow. "Are you serious?"

Jericho chuckled. "No. I've been a part of some checkpoints in my days working with both the army and the marines. As long as it looks real and Emily doesn't incriminate herself or break down, she'll get through the border. Trust me."

"This better work. Because if they get caught, we could ultimately lose our chance at getting V back. Or finding the flash drive. Or taking down Rajabi." Burke turned back around after making his point.

"Care to make a wager," Jericho said.

Burke turned to the side and said, "What's the bet?"

"If they make it through the checkpoint and the border, I get to fly one of the drones."

Burke laughed. "What are you, a child? It's not a toy."

"No. But I am the one with half a brain who concocted the plan that will get two covert agents over the border and into Syria. And I guess, in turn, the one who made the entire mission possible."

Jones turned toward Burke. "The guy does have a point, Burke."

Burke huffed. "Fine. But it's on you if you crash it."

"Hey," Jericho said and held up his hands, "I'll own that."

The phone rang and interrupted their conversation. Burke picked up. "Emily. What happened?"

"We made it through the first checkpoint."

Jericho clapped in the backseat, then mumbled, "Halfway there."

Burke shook off his comment and said, "What happened? What were they looking for?"

"Us."

Burke was thrown. "What do you mean?"

"I mean, they were looking for us. They didn't have pictures yet, but they were looking for two single women traveling alone."

"Then how did you get through?"

Emily laughed through the speaker. "The baby bump. Once we got out of the car, they saw that I was *very* pregnant, and they let us go."

Burke turned around and found Jericho's eyes.

Jericho laughed. "Works every time."

Burke breathed a sigh and said, "I'm so glad you made it through."

"Us too. Natasha says the next part is more of a formality. They just stamp our passports and let us through. Not too many people are trying to break into Syria. More of an issue getting back into Jordan."

"I imagine that's true."

"GPS has us in Damascus in a little over an hour," Emily said.

"Roger that. We'll get there a little before and find a safe place to do some reconnaissance, so we'll know if you're walking into a trap. And trust me, if you are, we'll be there to eliminate any threat."

"Thank you, Burke. And thank your guy for the pregnancy idea. It worked."

Burke saw the wide grin on Jericho's face. "He says you're welcome."

"I'll see you soon, Burke."

"See you soon."

CHAPTER TWENTY-NINE

As the sun beat down on Rajabi's face, he shielded his eyes to watch Cyrus from atop a wide staircase that moved away from his front doorstep. Cyrus and a group of ten others readied their vehicles and awaited their orders before piling into the convoy.

"Cyrus," Rajabi called, waving him over.

Cyrus slammed the car door shut and walked toward his boss. While Cyrus was walking, Rajabi watched Lopez through the windshield.

"Keep an eye on him." Rajabi nodded toward the vehicle. "I still don't trust him. And you remember what I told you. After he gives you the flash drive, kill him inside the building. Him and the girl. Do not bring them back here. Understood?"

Cyrus nodded. Then both men turned around and looked at Lopez. They could see he was still holding his hand, no doubt in severe pain from the knife wound. Even though they cauterized the injury and bandaged it, you could still see the blood soaking through the gauze.

"What if the girl alerted the CIA about the meeting?"

"I'm sure she did. Which is why I'm sending you in with so many more of my men."

Rajabi didn't have an army at his beck and call, but he did have enough men at his disposal to cover most threats.

Rajabi continued. "Once you arrive, sit back and wait. Do not stick too close. If an outsider sees you, I want them to question if you're together. Then wait to see if any infidel tries to follow them inside. And if someone does follow him into the building, I want you to take them down. Does that make sense?"

Cyrus nodded.

"Good. Now, go."

Cyrus turned and walked toward the car. Rajabi continued to watch them leave the compound. As soon as the last car disappeared, he took a lap around the perimeter of his property. He wanted to make sure every man guarding his residence was exactly where they were supposed to be.

When Rajabi reached the backyard, he looked out over the pool deck and was reminded of the dead man he had killed the day prior. He could still see the interrogation play out in his mind that led up to the man floating face down in his own blood.

The floating dead man was a friend and ally named Mustiel. Rajabi had relied on Mustiel to keep the flash drive secret. But over the previous few months, unbeknownst to Rajabi, Veronica had seduced Mustiel into giving her access to the drive, which is how she stole it in the first place. When Rajabi found out about the betrayal, he did not hesitate to kill him.

After shaking the memory away, Rajabi turned from the pool deck and walked back toward the house.

The end was coming near for Veronica, and he wanted to have one last act of power over her. He would grant her a wish—her last meal on earth.

When he arrived at the room where she was being held, he was met by two men standing guard outside the door. He nodded at each of them. One reached into his pocket and took out a key and then unlocked the door and stepped aside.

The room was pitch black with no natural light coming in from anywhere. He flipped on the light switch and watched Veronica curl into a ball and try to blink the brightness away.

As her eyes adjusted, Rajabi moved toward her. She was chained to a bed, and her hands were locked into cuffs. When her eyes adjusted and she saw Rajabi close, she recoiled even further, like she wanted to disappear into the mattress or even the wall behind her.

He breathed deep and looked at her. She was silent, and then he began, "I want you to know this before you die. You've been betrayed by your own country. By the CIA. They're not negotiating with me, and they're leaving you here to die in any way I see fit."

Veronica leaned back, then lurched forward and sent her saliva flying toward Rajabi's face. The spit drilled him in the eye, and some dripped down his nose. He reached up to wipe the spit away. "I will say this . . . you've got some spirit." Then he stood over her and took a powerful stance. "I only tell you this because as soon as Lopez gets his hands on the flash drive from your friend Natasha"—Veronica's eyes went wide—"That's right. She's on her way to meet Lopez as we speak. Together they're going to retrieve the flash drive and bring it to me. Once that happens, I'm afraid that your life, well, it doesn't mean anything anymore. So, I came here as a gesture of good faith to offer you one final meal. You name it. If we have it in the house, my chef will cook it for you—exactly to your liking."

Rajabi stared at her for another ten seconds before she spoke.

"I'd rather choke on my own vomit than eat anything you have to offer."

"That wouldn't be *my* first choice, but that can be arranged." Rajabi snapped his fingers, and the two men guarding the door appeared.

Veronica's breathing turned heavy as one man came near.

"No. Stop. Get away from me!" She kicked with her legs to try to halt his advance.

Just as he reached his arm back to punch her in the gut, Rajabi said, "I'm trying to be a good host here. I'll give you another chance. Take my food offer, or Jellel here, will make good on your original menu choice."

Veronica tucked her elbows close to her ribs so Jellel couldn't hit her. "Fine. Steak. Chicken. Fish. Whatever you have—just keep him away."

Rajabi snapped again, and the two men disappeared from the

room. Then he bent down to her bedside. "See, now, was that so hard?"

She gritted her teeth and moved her body away from his rancid breath. Then he stood and walked toward the door. Before he left the room, she had one request. "Can you please leave the lights on?"

He turned around and gave a sly grin. "Sure. Why not! After all, you won't be seeing much of anything once I get the call from Lopez that he has your flash drive."

CHAPTER THIRTY

The city of Damascus was a bustling metropolis, at least as far as Middle Eastern metropolises go. The city was highly populated and had thousands of structures. As Burke stared out the passenger-side window, he said, "This is not going to be easy."

"Did Emily give you any indication as to where the building was?" Jericho said from the backseat.

Burke shook his head. "Supposedly Lopez has that information, and he isn't going to give up the location until after Natasha arrives in Damascus."

"Smart man," Jericho said.

"Maybe, maybe not," Burke said.

"How do you mean?" Jones said.

"Well, we don't know for sure if he's flipped sides. It's only speculation. Natasha and Emily just had a bad feeling about him," Burke said.

"Since when do you go against a woman's intuition?" Jones said.

"Oh, I don't. Ever. Which is why I feel like this mission is so important. We all agree that Lopez's escape from the cemetery and then magical reappearance was odd, right?" Burke said.

All agreed.

"So what are we gonna do, drive around town until we get word from Emily?" Sammy said. "What if we end up on the opposite side of the city when the brakes fall off? How will we provide backup if we don't even know where they are?"

Jericho laughed. "That was like word vomit there, buddy. I don't know if I've ever heard you ask so many questions all at once."

Burke watched Sammy turn to look out the window.

Sammy said, "Maybe you should use fewer words and shut your mouth."

"Relax, big guy, I'm just messing with you." Jericho playfully hit him. "I agree with you. What's the plan here, Burke?"

"We get centralized. Then we wait for Emily's call."

"What happens if Lopez doesn't give Natasha the address to the building where the flash drive is?" Jericho said. "What if he tells her to meet him somewhere else so they can drive together to the new location? They'd be going in blind. And you promised them we would be there for backup."

"Emily is smart," Burke said. "She knows all this. She knows how to play the spy games just as well as anyone else."

"I hope so, Burke. For her sake and the others," Jericho said.

Burke turned around and faced Jones. They didn't say anything, but their concerned look told enough of the story.

Natasha drove from the south into the outskirts of Damascus. She looked over at Emily and said, "I think it's time we call Lopez."

"Agreed," Emily said.

Natasha took out her phone and dialed his number. He picked up on the first ring. "Hello," he said weakly.

"Lopez, is that you?"

He coughed into the phone, and Natasha shuddered from the sound.

"You all right?" Natasha asked.

"Fine. It's just—"

"Just what?" Natasha asked.

"Never mind."

Natasha curled her lip and continued, "We're in Damascus. On the south side of the city."

"You made it through the border then?" He sounded half shocked and half relieved.

"Obviously. But not without difficulty."

"I find that to be the case on most border crossings in the Middle East."

They shared a laugh. Even though Lopez's laugh seemed more forced.

Their conversation was going nowhere fast, which seemed unusual. Natasha needed to get to the point. "Where am I going, Lopez?"

"The Al-Mazza Municipality. Do you know it?"

"Not really. Is that on the eastern side of the city?"

"West. Drive in that direction. Call me back when you're close, and I'll give you more instructions."

"Wait. Lopez?" Natasha yelled louder than she should have, but she didn't want him to hang up.

"What is it, Natasha?"

She looked over at Emily. Emily could tell she wanted to ask the question. After all, she was likely wondering the same thing.

"What's with all the secrecy? Why not just tell me where I'm going? Don't you trust me?"

There was silence on the other end. Nothing but static. The line went dead, and he was gone.

Emily stared at Natasha. "What was that about?"

"He's with someone," Natasha said. "He couldn't give us the address because someone doesn't want us to have the upper hand. If only Lopez knows where we're going, then we and Burke can't make a move on them. I don't want to have to say this, but . . . we're likely being led into a trap."

Emily sat back against her seat and stared out the window. She inhaled through her nose and spoke to herself. "Burke will want to know about this."

"Call him," Natasha said. "See what he wants us to do."

"It's Emily." Burke showed Jones the phone. "Emily, are you close?"

"We're on the southern end of Damascus."

"Glad to hear it. Did you get in touch with Lopez."

"We did."

"And? Did he give you the location?"

"Al-Mazza Municipality. But then we wait for further instructions."

Burke turned away from the phone and said to Jones, "You got that?"

"Got it," Jones said.

Burke came back to the phone. "Further instructions? This sounds off."

"Yeah, and . . ."

"And what?" Burke said.

"Natasha and I think we're walking into a trap."

Burke held his breath. Deep down, he knew that was the most likely scenario as well.

"Burke, you there?" Burke could tell she did not appreciate his silence.

"I am. And yes, sounds like a trap for sure."

"What should we do?"

Burke put his hand to his chin and began devising a plan. Some possible way that Emily and Natasha could break free if they were in fact taken. But every scenario he considered led to the same outcome for Emily, Natasha, and Lopez.

"Look, Emily, what I'm about to tell you is imperative. You need to listen to everything I say."

"Burke, your tone is scaring me."

"That's the last thing you need to be frightened of at this point."

"You knew this was going to happen this way, didn't you?" Emily said.

"I had my suspicions. But I hoped I was wrong."

Burke could hear her take a disappointing sigh. "Okay, what do you want us to do?"

"Believe it or not, Damascus is the best place for this to happen."

"Why?"

"Because there will be closed-circuit cameras everywhere. And we know someone who is adept at hacking into CCTV, don't we?"

Without hesitation, Emily said, "Lily."

"You know it. If we can't get to you in time, Lily will be able to track your movements. Even if you have to change vehicles, like I believe you might."

"That's a relief," Emily said.

"It is, but that's not all."

"Okay . . . ," Emily said.

"Lopez is only expecting Natasha, correct? Or did you tell him that you were coming along for the ride?"

"No. He only thinks Natasha will be there."

"Okay, so why are you with her?"

"What do you mean?" Emily said.

"I mean, you're either going to have to get out of the car and Natasha will need to go at this alone, or you'll have to come up with a story as to why you're with her. Because as soon as Lopez sees that you're together, he's going to suspect that we're on to him because Natasha has a tagalong."

"Okay," Emily said. "Do you have any suggestions for my storyline?"

"I don't. But either you need to either figure out a good one or you get out now and let her go alone."

"I'm not leaving her, Burke. Would you, if you were in my shoes?"

"No chance."

"That's what I thought."

"Then take those next ten miles and come up with something Lopez, and the men he'll likely have with him, will believe."

"You think he'll have men with him?"

"If not at his side, then close by watching. No way Rajabi would let Lopez out of his sight if he has flipped him."

"That's comforting," Emily joked.

"It's not meant to be. Remember what I told you in Utah. You have to be comfortable in uncomfortable situations."

"Oh, I remember," Emily said.

"Good. Now, go over your story, and . . ."

"And what?"

Burke wanted to tell her to be careful, but instead, he said, "Keep us updated on your whereabouts."

"Roger that, Burke."

"Good-bye, Emily."

Burke hung up the phone and stared out the windshield. He prayed silently to himself. And deep down he hoped that wasn't the last conversation he would ever have with Emily.

CHAPTER THIRTY-ONE

Jones drove east toward the Al-Mazza Municipality. They were about fifteen miles from that region of Damascus. The city was not unlike many cities in the United States. There were hotels, restaurants, shopping areas, the perfect place to blend in with the masses. Maybe if they could get there before Emily and Natasha, even before Lopez, they could get lucky by happening on them as they came together. But as Burke knew, luck had nothing to do with it.

"Any guesses as to where Lopez will be leading Natasha and Emily?" Jones asked.

All shook their heads. None of them was familiar with the city.

"My gut tells me he's gonna stay off the main roads, but he'll want to meet someplace public," Burke said. "Maybe a park, a lake, or a school . . . check the GPS on your phones while I reach out to Lily to fill her in."

Both Jericho and Sammy did as they were instructed while Burke called Lily.

"Burke," Lily whispered.

Burke heard the hesitancy in her voice. "Why are you whispering?"

"'Cause Stallone's looking for me."

"Does he know we're gone?"

"Of course he does. That's why he's after me. He knows I know something."

"Where are you right now?"

"In your room."

Burke was thrown. "*My* room? Why?"

"Because I like the smell. By the way, what cologne do you use?"

"Wait, what?"

Lily snapped back to answer his original question. "What do you mean *why*? Where else would I go?"

"That's the first place Stallone will look when he can't find you anywhere else in the compound."

"Then where would you like me to go? We're at a black site in the middle of Syria. It's not like I can head to the nearest Starbucks and use their Wi-Fi."

Burke pictured the base, imagined every possible hiding spot.

"What about Mack?"

"What about him?"

"Have you been in to see him?"

"No. Why would I go there? He's in the infirmary."

"Exactly. That's where you need to hide out. If Stallone comes sniffing, Mack will throw him off your scent. And he can help you. He'll know our tactics, and that'll give you an advantage when you're trying to figure out our next steps."

"Good thinking, Burke."

He could hear her moving.

"I'll call you back when I'm there," she said.

Just as she hung up, Jericho spoke up from the backseat. "Found a park, Burke. It's in the middle of the Al-Mazza."

"What about access points, roads in and out?"

Jericho lowered his head and zoomed in on the screen. "Yeah. Two ways in and out."

"That's where I'd go," Burke said to himself. "Jericho, give Jonesy your phone so he can put us on the right track. I just hope we're not too late."

Natasha turned onto the Beirut Highway and headed west toward Al-Mazza. They were getting close and still didn't have a plan.

"Maybe it's best I drop you off before we get there," Natasha said. "I can handle Lopez."

"No." Emily held up her hand. "That's out of the question. I'm not leaving you alone. We're in this together."

"Then what are we going to tell Lopez?"

Emily breathed in deep and thought for a moment. Then words seemed to fall out of her mouth. "We tell him that you don't trust him."

"What do you mean?"

"I mean, tell him the truth. Tell him that him being alive is difficult to reconcile in your mind. Tell him you think he had help, that you can't trust him, and I'm here as your backup."

"What if Rajabi's men are with him? What if they interfere and break us apart?"

Emily stared at her. "That won't happen."

Natasha scrunched her brow, confused. "How do you know that?"

Instead of coming back with an answer, Emily posed a question. "What's Rajabi's end goal in all this?"

Natasha was taken aback. "The flash drive."

"Exactly. He's not going to risk you getting scared off. Remember, you're the one with the power here. Sure, Lopez has the location, but you hold the button in your hand, and Lopez can't enter the building without you saying so. Rajabi knows that too. He's not going to harm you, me, or even Lopez until he gets what he wants."

"Yeah, I suppose you're right."

"Of course I'm right," Emily said, smiling at her own cleverness. "Sometimes, though, it just takes some time to put all the pieces together."

They both laughed, and then Natasha said, "Should I call him? We're coming up on the city now."

Emily nodded, and Natasha took out her phone. As she dialed the number, Emily warned her, "Do not tell him I'm with you. That needs to be a surprise when we get there."

Natasha nodded as Lopez answered the call.

"Hello," Lopez said.

"I'm here," Natasha said.

"There's a park in the middle of the city. I'm sending you a pin now. Meet me there in five minutes. I'll be waiting." He ended the call.

Burke felt his phone vibrate. It was Lily. "Are you with Mack?" Burke said.

"No, not yet. Had to take a detour. Stallone was close."

"Okay. Call me when you're there. I need you to link up with CCTV. It's a matter of life and—"

"Hold on, Burke. Someone's com—" The line went dead.

Burke dropped his phone in his lap and looked at Jones. "If she gets caught and Stallone takes her computer away, Emily's as good as dead." Burke's heart was in his throat, and his chest heaved up and down. "How much longer?" Burke yelled.

"GPS says ten minutes," Jones said. "No wait. Now twelve."

Burke scratched his head. His anxiety level was rising, and there was nothing he could do to stop it. He felt trapped. Claustrophobic. He'd felt this before. He needed to calm down before he was sent into a panic. He closed his eyes and clenched his fists and took several deep breaths, in through the nose and out through the mouth.

"You okay, Burke?" Jones asked.

"Fine. Can you get there any faster?" Burke said.

Jones handed him the phone. Burke looked at the map. There was no way around, and the time changed from twelve to fifteen minutes.

Burke pounded the dashboard. "Damn it."

There was nothing he could do. His only hope was that Emily and Natasha had come up with a believable story. Something that wouldn't scare off Lopez or get them killed.

CHAPTER THIRTY-TWO

NATASHA FOLLOWED THE PIN ON HER PHONE. SHE HAD ONE MORE left turn, and then she would arrive at her destination. When she made the turn, Emily stared out her window to see four high-rise buildings spanning the block to the east. Each with the same height, length, and drab off-white color. It was some sort of apartment complex, and the park sat directly behind it.

As they continued to drive, more of the same buildings presented themselves, almost completely encircling the park itself, which must have been owned by the complex, a place to play for the children who lived there.

The parking lot directly in front of them was mostly empty. There were only about ten vehicles filling fifty spaces.

"I'm guessing he wants to meet us there." Emily pointed to the lot.

Natasha drove into an empty parking space and shifted her car into park. Both women leaned forward and stared out the windshield toward the park. In an open green space, four kids were kicking a soccer ball around. Beyond them were the swing set and playground equipment. No sign of Lopez.

Natasha's gaze turned to the right, and Emily's eyes moved in the same direction. Emily searched the lot for any man inside a vehicle, but every car or truck sat empty.

"Where is he?" Natasha said.

Before Emily could answer, Natasha's phone rang.

She and Emily jumped in their seats.

Natasha lifted the phone and looked at Emily.

"Answer it," Emily encouraged her.

"Hello."

"What's with the other girl?"

"*He knows you're here,*" Natasha mouthed.

Emily rolled her hands and encouraged her to tell him the story they had previously rehearsed.

"She's my protection," Natasha said.

"Protection from who?" Lopez said.

"From you."

"Why do you need protection from me? We were supposed to do this together. V said—"

"I know what V said," Natasha said, cutting him off. "You don't have to remind me. In fact, you're lucky I even agreed to this. V was supposed to be here, to enter that building with you. Not you alone. And certainly not with me."

"Easy, easy," Lopez said.

"Besides, we thought you were dead. And why you're not certainly seems . . ."

"Seems what?"

"Strange, to say the least. Which is why I brought a friend. She's here to make sure you don't turn on me."

Lopez paused, then said, "Fair enough. Bring the girl. But I'm going to need you to ditch the car."

Emily's eyes went wide as she stared at Natasha. She wanted to say no, but what choice did they have?

Burke, you better be watching this, she thought. *Where are you?* She looked out the windows for any sign of him.

"What do you mean, ditch the car?" Natasha was stalling.

"Exactly what I said. Get out of the vehicle and walk across the park. Walk along the path. I'm parked under the trees on the east end."

"What? Where?"

Natasha leaned further forward to get a better look out the windshield, but the park was long, about two hundred yards across. No way she could see him without a spotting scope or binoculars.

"You won't be able to see me. You'll just have to trust me. Get out now. You and the girl. And walk toward the opposite end of the parking lot."

Emily nodded and grabbed her phone—the battery was almost dead, but she needed to send Burke her location pin with the words, "*Leaving the car behind. Riding with Lopez.*"

Natasha looked down at Emily's hands to make sure she was finished typing. Then she told Lopez, "Okay, we're coming now."

Both women grabbed their packs from the backseat and then opened their respective doors and stepped into the fresh air.

The park was shaped like a triangle with the base being the parking lot. Natasha led Emily toward the concrete path that surrounded the open field. As they walked, Emily shifted her head slightly side to side, looking for any threats or possible signs of Burke.

"Take it slow," Emily whispered from behind Natasha.

How slow could they possibly go without looking like they were stalling on purpose? As much as Lopez needed Natasha to keep her finger off the detonator, the CIA needed the location of the flash drive even more.

Halfway down the length of the park, both women witnessed Lopez exit a vehicle. He was alone, but that didn't mean someone else wasn't watching.

The roar of the children's laughter turned the women's attention toward the playground. The moment Emily saw the children, she was transported back to the presidential compound in Nigeria. Children brought a smile to her face. Always had. Maybe even more so since that fateful day with Burke. It had made her want to protect them more, even if they weren't her responsibility.

They were less than a hundred feet from Lopez's car. Emily leaned close and whispered into Natasha's ear, "Once we get inside the car with him, don't speak. Do everything you can to look out the window. Lean against the window if you can. I want to give Lily every possible angle of our faces so she can pick us up on CCTV."

Fifty feet.

"He's smart," Emily said. "Parked under a tree to avoid satellite imagery."

When they arrived at the car, both women stopped.

"What's in the bags?" he said.

"Change of clothes," Natasha said.

"Any weapons?" Lopez said.

Natasha looked toward Emily. She wanted her to be the one to make the call on what to say.

"Two Glocks," Emily said. "And don't forget the button to blow the C4."

Lopez lifted his hand and pointed behind them. "Toss the Glocks in the trash."

They noticed the blood-soaked bandage around Lopez's pinky finger.

"What happened to your hand?" Natasha said.

Emily stepped back toward the can. Natasha's question was just the distraction she needed—she emptied the clothes into the trash but kept the Glocks in the bottom of the pack.

"What? This?" He held up his hand. "This is what Saam Rajabi is capable of." He tore the gauze away to showcase his missing pinky finger.

Natasha grimaced at the sight of the blood, but not Emily.

"When did he do that?" Emily wanted to see if his timeline matched up.

"Yesterday. After he caught up to us and tortured us."

Emily didn't buy it. "And it looks like it's still bleeding now. Seems like a much fresher wound than that."

Lopez sneered at her but simply said, "Get in and let's go."

The women shared a look of concern before dropping inside the vehicle. Then Emily turned around and thought, *Burke, you better be watching this.* But he wasn't. And neither was Lily.

CHAPTER THIRTY-THREE

JONES WEAVED IN AND OUT OF TRAFFIC ON HIS WAY DOWN BEIRUT Highway.

"It's just up here," Burke said. "Take the next exit, then it's your first left."

Jones followed Burke's instructions. He was driving faster than he should have, but Burke wasn't going to be the one to tell him to slow down. After receiving Emily's text about riding with Lopez only two minutes prior, there was still a chance they might be able to chase them down. Maybe see Emily or Natasha enter Lopez's car before they drove away from the park.

After taking the exit and turning left, Jones looked to Burke for the next instruction. "Now where?"

"There." Burke pointed across the street. "The pin is literally on the other side of those apartment buildings."

Without slowing down, Jones yanked the wheel to the left.

"There it is," Burke yelled.

Jones sped into the parking lot and parked in the vacant spot next to Natasha's stolen sedan. They all hopped out of the vehicle. Burke stood and spun in a circle, searching for any sign of the two women.

"See anything, Jonesy?" Burke shouted over the roof.

"I got nothing."

Burke slammed his hand on the hood of the SUV and stared at the phone in his other hand. He was on top of thc pin. He moved toward the car parked next to him and peered inside the windows. There it was. On the passenger seat. Emily's phone was just sitting there. A sign she'd left for Burke and another way to track her location.

"It's her phone, Jonesy," Burke said and turned back toward the park. "We search the park. Maybe they're on the opposite side hiding someplace."

Each man stared at Burke, but none moved. They knew it was a fool's errand. Deep down, they knew Emily was gone.

"You heard him. Move," Jones said.

Jericho and Sammy broke away and walked out into the grassy open area and split left. Jones stayed behind to have a word with Burke.

"Don't worry, Burke, we'll find her," Jones said.

"I hope you're right, Jonesy."

"I know I am."

Burke and Jones split right to mirror the other men's movements in the opposite direction. There were fewer trees on Burke's side of the park. This meant less shade and a clearer vantage point across the park.

Burke continued down the path along the perimeter. He looked past the children on the playground and saw that he had caught up with Jericho and Sammy walking on the other side.

They were coming to the same point. A vertex between the two paths. All of them stopped at once and stared at the road. Many cars passed by, but still no sign of Emily.

"Look around. She had to be here. See if she left us a clue," Burke said. He felt a buzz in his pocket. He lifted his phone, and it was Lily. "Finally. Tell me you're with Mack."

"I am. And I hacked into CCTV."

"Do you have eyes on Emily?" Burke's voice went up.

"No."

Burke's shoulders slumped.

"Where are you?" Lily said.

"At a park in the Al-Mazza Municipality in Damascus."

"Okay, let me see what I can find."

"Emily texted me the pin. This is where they met Lopez."

"Can you text me that location?" Lily said. "That way I can lock onto the cameras in the area and rewind the footage."

"You can do that?" Burke said and sent his location her way.

Lily laughed on the other end. "Ye of little faith. There aren't many things I can't do with computers."

Suddenly, Jericho called out, "I got something here, Burke."

"Hold on a sec, Lily," he said as he headed toward Jericho.

Jericho lifted some woman's clothes from a nearby trash can, including a sweatshirt that said *Duke Soccer*. Jericho put them to his nose. "Freshly washed. Not something you would throw away for no reason."

"Got it, Burke," he heard Lily say. "I'm in."

"In where?" Burke turned away from Jericho and looked back across the street.

"CCTV," Lily said. "Burke, do you see any stationary cameras across the street from you?"

"No." Burke searched the corners of the tall apartment buildings. "Wait, yeah, there's one there." He kept searching. "And another. Two more—they're everywhere."

"That's what I like to hear," Lily said. "This might be a shot in the dark, Burke, but can you tell where she might have been picked up?"

"Jericho just found some women's clothes in the trash can right by the road."

"Okay, but that doesn't really tell us much, other than some lady may have gotten sick of her wardrobe and tossed it in the nearest trash."

"Don't think so. I mean, I never saw Emily wear the sweatshirt, but there was a grey hoodie with *Duke Soccer* etched across the front. I think Emily is trying to leave us bread crumbs."

"That's where Emily went to college, right?" Lily said.

"Veronica too," Burke reminded her.

"That's right. Then that has to be something," Lily said.

"Maybe Lopez made them dump their gear."

"Hold on, let me see if your theory holds any water," Lily said.

"What's she saying?" Jones said.

Burke held up his finger and waited for an answer.

"Got 'em, Burke."

"Nice," Burke said. "She found them." He told the men off the phone.

"Right next to where you said."

Burke started walking back toward their car. He waved the others to follow him. As Lily gave him more insight, he picked up the pace and moved into a full sprint across the park.

By the time they arrived back at the SUV, Lily had given them a rundown. She told Burke that they had traveled north of the park and away from the neighborhood.

"Lily, I can't thank you enough. You've likely saved her life."

"Let's not get ahead of ourselves here, Burke. Once they're out of the neighborhood, I won't be able to track them via closed-circuit cameras. I'll need access to satellite imagery."

"Can you get access?"

"Of course, but . . ." she trailed off.

"But what?" Burke said.

"If this goes south and Stallone finds out I hacked an NSA satellite, well, then we're not only talking about my departure from the agency, but also potential jail time for violating countless acts of espionage."

"You and me both, Lily," Burke said. "You and me both." He ducked into the SUV. "Just get me their location. Do whatever it takes."

CHAPTER THIRTY-FOUR

EMILY LEANED AGAINST THE WINDOW IN THE BACKSEAT ON THE driver's side. With Natasha sitting shotgun, she wanted to give Lily the best chance at proof of life through CCTV. As they drove, there were so many questions Emily wanted to ask, but she kept them all to herself.

Instead, she paid attention to every turn Lopez made on the short trip. She knew they were heading north and out of the Al-Mazza Municipality, and as soon as Lopez made the next turn, Emily peered over her shoulder to see if anyone was following them. Two other vehicles mirrored their movements. One was a panel van, the other a dark-colored SUV that could have held at least six full-grown men.

She reached down at the bag at her feet and stuck her hand inside. She watched Lopez's eyes in the rearview. He was focused on the turn, which allowed her the ability to lift one of the Glocks from the bag. She rested the handgun under her leg and sat back against the seat just as Lopez found her eyes in the mirror.

Emily shifted her attention to the back of Natasha's head. She wondered if Natasha saw the cars following them as well. If so, would she see the mission through? Would she let Lopez inside the building?

Before they reached Damascus, they didn't discuss in detail what they'd do if Lopez had extra men at the building. They had relied—maybe too much—on Burke—and his promise to be their savior.

"We're here," Lopez said, making one final turn.

Emily leaned forward and peered through the windshield to see that they were approaching a new municipality—a neighborhood much like the one they had just left behind. This time, though, there was no park with buildings all around. On the south side of the road stood a lone building that was under construction. And beyond the building to the south was nothing but dirt and rock extending for miles back toward the Al-Mazza Municipality. On the opposite side of the street were occupied buildings. Cars lined the parking lot, and people were rushing around like it was any normal day.

The unfinished building site was not what Emily had imagined in her head when she saw the live video feed from inside Natasha's apartment in Amman.

"This is it?" Natasha said.

Apparently, it wasn't what Natasha expected either.

"Not what you expected?" Lopez said.

After Lopez brought the car to a stop in a nearby parking spot, Emily leaned forward and grabbed the Glock, and as she stepped outside, she tucked the gun into her belt and folded her shirt over before Lopez saw it.

Emily looked both ways and saw cars approaching from either direction. This was a bustling area. Why Veronica and Lopez had chose this section of town to hide the flash drive was beyond her comprehension.

"Why did you and V choose to hide the flash drive here?"

"First off, it already had the security cameras in place because it was under construction. But we'd been watching the site for weeks. We even went as far as contacting the municipality about its completion. There were some problems that halted production, and it wasn't set to be finished until late next year. We knew the building would be a safe spot to leave the flash drive before we could return and retrieve it. The building was close enough to Rajabi's compound, and it was unlikely anyone would be coming in and out if we had to dump it and run. Hence V's instructions to you."

Emily scrunched her brow. "That's a big risk. What about homeless people . . . or squatters? Anyone could've have just walked inside."

Lopez grinned and said, "Besides the cameras, the doors are chained shut. And only *I* have access." He held up the key. "That was the two-part scenario." Finally, Emily understood why both Lopez and V needed to be at the building. "V trusted me to hold it." He looked at Natasha. "So what do you say? Do you believe me now?"

She looked at Emily for confirmation. Both shared a look but didn't say anything. Natasha simply nodded, and Lopez turned his attention to the roadway and waited for the cars to pass by, then sprinted across the street. Emily and Natasha followed close on his heels. When he reached the front door, he inserted the key into the bottom of the padlock.

"How did you guys get a key to the building anyway?" Emily asked.

Once he unlatched the lock and the chain from the front door, he smiled. "V is very persuasive. She had the man at the municipality eating out of her hand. Much like she did when she was able to seduce Rajabi's man for access to the flash drive. The guy told her she reminded him of Scarlett Johansson. He handed the key over for the chance at a date with an American woman—the fool."

Once the chain was unraveled from the door, Lopez opened it. "Shall we?" He held the door for the women. Natasha walked through first, but Emily hesitated and looked back toward the street for any sign of Burke or the two vehicles she saw following them before. Those two vehicles were nowhere in sight, but neither was Burke.

Burke, where are you? She scanned from building to building, hoping to catch sight of him, but she saw nothing.

If she had learned anything from him, she knew that circumstances in the field are all about being comfortable in uncomfortable situations. So she decided to take charge in the moment. "After you. I insist."

Lopez stepped through the open door, and she followed close behind. If she was truly on her own with no backup, then she did not want to turn her back on him—not even for a second. As she walked behind Lopez, she reached behind her back and lifted the tail of her shirt and grabbed the handle of the Glock.

She was ready for him to make a move—she was ready for anything.

CHAPTER THIRTY-FIVE

"All right, Burke, I just saw them on satellite walking into a building north of Al-Mazza Municipality," Lily said.

"How far north of us?" Burke asked Lily. He pointed though the windshield and instructed Jones on where to go. "Turn here. Lily says go north."

Jones exited Beirut Highway and wound around a cloverleaf and onto an unmarked road.

"You're sure, Burke?" Jones said. "This doesn't look like it leads anywhere."

"Just stay on the road, Jonesy. Lily can see the exact route they took."

"You got it."

Lily came back over the phone and told Burke that their location was less than five miles away.

"It's five miles, Jonesy," Burke said.

"Okay, I see you on the satellite," Lily said. "Stay on your path until you reach an overpass. You'll go under the overpass and then head west for one mile. Then the building will be on your left-hand side."

"Copy that, Lily. Are there other buildings around the site?"

"Yes," Lily said.

"How many?"

"Hold on. Let me count." She mumbled off a five count, and then Burke cut her off.

"There are multiple?" Burke said.

"Yeah . . ." She trailed off, and Burke overheard Mack talking in the background.

"What's Mack saying?"

"He's telling me there are a few good tactical positions you could use for cover as you look for threats in the area."

"That's my guy." Burke pumped his fist.

Lily continued. "He also said there are a couple of vehicles you should be aware of that just stopped across the street from the building."

"Is anyone getting out?"

"Not yet, but Mack is taking a closer look. It's hard to see from the satellite images."

"Can you hack the building's security cameras?" Burke said.

"Sure, but then I'd lose sight of the satellite images from above. I didn't know if you wanted me to do that. Right now I have a much better vantage point of the two stopped vehicles from overhead than I would from the closed-circuit cameras on the side of the building."

"Gotcha."

"Even more than that, if and when Emily leaves with Natasha and Lopez, I'll definitely need the satellite view."

"Okay," Burke said. "Just stay with the overhead view for now."

Lily gave Burke the cross-street reference point.

"Thanks, Lily," Burke said.

"You got it."

"Keep me updated about their movements. If you or Mack see anything before they exit the building, call me. Understood?"

"Got it, Burke."

Jones drove precisely to the cross street that Mack had suggested. He stopped the vehicle at a high-rise about five hundred feet before the building Emily and the others had entered. Burke jumped out of the passenger side and moved to the back of the hatchback. He grabbed his bag and lifted out one of the drones.

Jericho turned around in the backseat, looked Burke in the eye, and said, "Don't forget about your promise."

Burke grinned. "Right. I'm gonna give you access to the only thing we have with the potential to see what kind of trap Emily and Natasha might be walking into."

"You gave your word," Jericho said.

Burke cast off his childish quip about the drone. "Sure thing, bud."

Burke lifted the drone into the air and reentered the SUV to get out of the daylight and back into the cover of the vehicle. The drone took off high into the air and showcased the fifteen stories of the building in front of them. It climbed over the blaze-orange rooftop and moved west.

Jericho and Sammy leaned in from the backseat and watched the screen as Burke flew the drone westward. It only took a few seconds before it hovered over the two vehicles in question.

"Wait, what if the guys inside those vehicles hear the drone hovering? Won't that make too much noise?" Jericho said.

"No. I put it in safety mode. Brings down the noise to almost silent. Think, a hummingbird's wings," Burke said. "The only risk is sight. But even so, the drone looks like any other drone on the market. Could be just some random kid flying it around for fun."

"That's crazy," Sammy said.

Burke continued to fly the drone above the vehicles, but he still couldn't get a visual on the men inside. "Jericho, I'll let you do the honors. Just so you can't say I didn't let you try." Jericho scooted forward on his seat and reached his hand toward the screen. "You ready?" Jericho nodded. "Then it's time to go thermal." Burke instructed Jericho to tap the green button on the screen. Suddenly, the screen lit up reddish orange. "That's . . ." Burke counted the men in vehicle one, then moved on to the second. Once he finished counting, he found Jones's eyes and moaned, "That's ten."

Jericho and Sammy fell hard against the backseat.

"Ten men?" Jericho said. "In the middle of the day. In the middle of some random neighborhood in Damascus."

"Yeah, sucks," Burke said.

"Sucks? That's all you got . . . *sucks*?"

Burke narrowed his eyes. "Emily's counting on us. You know how this ends for her and Natasha after they get the flash drive, right?"

Jericho nodded. "With two bullets to the chest and one in the head."

"That's if they're lucky," Jones added.

"A lot worse could happen too," Burke said. "Who's to say the hit squad in the trucks don't make a messy video of their deaths."

"That's quite the imagination, Burke," Sammy said. "We don't even know if the men in those trucks are here for Emily and Natasha."

Burke shifted his gaze from Jericho and turned it on Sammy. It was true. Burke didn't have that proof, but he did have his gut. And that rarely let him down.

"Look, I'm not saying we shouldn't do this. I'm just thinking about the repercussions if this goes sideways," Sammy said.

Burke knew full well what would happen if this didn't go according to plan. And Jones could sense his friend was lost in that thought.

"What are you thinking?" Jones said.

"Well, the last time I defied an order, it didn't exactly turn out well, did it, Jonesy?"

"No, it did not. Even if I tried to warn you about it," Jones said.

"Uh, excuse me, care to fill us in?" Jericho piped up from the back. "What exactly are we talking about here?"

Burke looked at him and grinned. "That's classified."

Jones and Burke shared a laugh; then Jones said, "So, what, you want to call Stallone? Get his permission?"

"Uh . . . ," Jericho started.

"I don't see any other play here," Burke said. "I'm usually the guy who acts first and begs for forgiveness, rather than seeking permission, but this . . . this could be just the act of aggression that Stallone and the president are trying to avoid during the Israeli conflict."

"What if he tells us to stand down?" Jones said.

Burke eyed his friend, then gave a subtle grin. "I won't ask you three to come with me, but you know me—I'm not leaving her to die.

I'll walk right into that building. Put three into Lopez and walk out the back door with both women *and* the flash drive."

Jones laughed at his brashness.

"So then, what's the point in asking Stallone?" Jericho said.

Burke nodded. "No point at all, but . . ."

CHAPTER THIRTY-SIX

EMILY CONTINUED TO FOLLOW LOPEZ AS HE WALKED TOWARD THE staircase at the back of the building. When Natasha reached out for Emily's hand, Emily took it and could sense her shaking and feel the sweat. Emily wanted to say something to calm her nerves, but she felt anxious too. She wondered what Burke would do to cut the tension, but her thoughts soon faded after she pictured herself beating Lopez to a bloody pulp if he tried to betray them.

Lopez spun around. "Are you ready to climb?"

Emily looked up to see the staircase extending all the way up to the top floor. She gulped the lump of spit that had formed in her mouth. Emily never liked climbing half-finished staircases. A memory of her father flashed in her mind, where he had to catch her when she'd almost fallen from an unfinished staircase at a work site. She joined him on countless jobs when she was a girl. He'd started his own contracting business after retiring from the marines.

She sighed. "How far up are we going?"

"All the way to the top." Lopez took the first step.

Emily and Natasha shared a worried look. They followed him up the staircase anyway. With every step, Emily stared upward, doing her best not to look through the unfinished stairs.

"So where exactly did you hide the flash drive?" Natasha said.

"In a hole. In the ventilation system. On the top floor."

Emily decided to ask a question that had been on her mind ever since she found out V was CIA. "Speaking of, why did Rajabi even put this information on a flash drive? Why not just store it in the cloud?"

"I assume because any good CIA analyst could hack into his computer and take what was on it."

Lily's face immediately flew into Emily's mind, and Emily knew he was right.

"So, what *is* on it?"

"The flash drive?" Lopez said.

"No, the Watergate tapes," Emily said. "Of course the flash drive. What's so important that Rajabi would be willing to kill you over it?"

"Secrets," he said.

"That's a little vague, don't you think?" Emily said. thought to herself. *Does he even know? She* thought to herself.

As Lopez turned the corner of the stairs to walk onto the platform, he glanced back at Emily and said, "That's need to know."

As he ascended, Emily said, "Cute. I think we've earned the right to know."

He stopped to face them both. "All right, along with the locations of many terrorist cells and their weapon caches, there are names."

Emily scrunched her brow. "Names? What names?"

Lopez sighed and started to climb again. "Maybe yours. Maybe mine, V's, Natasha's—who knows."

Natasha grabbed his arm as he walked. "Wait, why would my name be on the flash drive?"

Lopez eyed her, then looked at Emily. "V and I didn't get to that part. We were never able to see all the names. We alerted the director when we found the locations of terror groups. But we were immediately on the run from Rajabi after we took the flash drive. We only had time to scan the contents before we had to hide it here. We couldn't be caught at the border. There are way too many lives at stake."

"So why not just send the documents via encrypted email to the director with all the necessary information while you were on the run?" Emily said.

"V thought it would be too risky, and as both of you are aware, she has some trust issues. Even with people in our own government. The flash drive is the only copy. It's the only way to connect Rajabi to other terror groups. And his . . ." Lopez trailed off.

"His what?" Emily said, forcing him to continue.

Lopez's head fell.

"Spit it out, man," Emily said.

When he looked back up, he said, "Well, I suppose it's Rajabi's safety net against the other groups."

"What do you mean?" Natasha said.

"Rajabi's a businessman. He doesn't really fly under any sort of flag or regime. Sure, he was part of Hamas for a time, but during his time, he did it for his own benefit. To come to his own power and then break away. He still has allies throughout most of the Middle East, in most of the well-known terror groups as well as the lesser-known ones."

"Is this what you've learned over the past few years since you and V have been surveilling him?"

"That's right." He nodded.

Digesting all the information, Emily wondered why Lopez was telling them all this. Was it to throw them off his scent and make believe he wasn't the man they assumed he was? Maybe he *was* there to retain the flash drive with honorable intentions. Only time would tell.

When they reached the top floor, Lopez stopped to catch his breath. Emily was thankful. She was winded, and Natasha seemed to be also.

Emily took in some air to steady her breathing. "So where is it?"

"There." Lopez pointed through the floor-to-ceiling metal studs toward the opposite side of the room. "Just inside that vent hole."

They cut through the room faster by stepping through the metal studs. Lopez neared the opposite wall and reached through an opening.

Emily could see the strain on his face as he struggled.

"Almost there," he said as he reached. "Almost got it." Then he ripped his arm out of the hole and winced.

"What is it?" Emily said.

"I can't get my arm through the hole. My wrists are too wide. It's getting caught before I can get my hand through. That's why V needed to be the one to grab this. Her arms are smaller."

Emily stepped toward the hole. She did her best to see into the hole itself, but there was little light shining inside. "Flashlight?" she asked Lopez.

He shrugged. "No, sorry."

Emily looked at Natasha, but she, too, was empty-handed.

Emily sighed and stepped toward the wall and reached her arm inside the opening, but she quickly yanked it out and pointed her finger at Lopez. "Do not try anything. We're taking you on your honor here."

"You don't trust me?" Lopez held his chest. "Why would you not? V does. That's why we're here."

Emily curled her lip. To that point, he hadn't done anything for her not to trust him. She reached inside the hole again. "What am I supposed to be feeling here?" she said.

"There's a gap. Not much bigger than your arm. And then once you're through ,you should feel the drive stuck to the ductwork with some tape."

Emily did as she was instructed. Her fingers danced around the tin until she felt the rigidness of tape. "I think I feel it," she said. "Yeah, yeah, I got something." And just as she ripped it from its stuck place, she heard a yelp and then a scream.

Emily whipped around and in the same movement ripped the Glock from her belt line. She saw that Lopez was holding a gun to the side of Natasha's head and using her as a human shield.

CHAPTER THIRTY-SEVEN

BURKE HANDED THE REMOTE CONTROL TO JONES AND TOLD HIM TO fly the drone over the building to see if he could get eyes on Emily and the others while he made the call to Stallone. Burke only had one way to contact him, and it was through Lily. She would need to come out of hiding and track down the old man.

"Burke," Lily said right away, "what's happening? I see you on the satellite. Were you able to get more intel on the vehicles, or get eyes on Emily and Lopez?"

"Can you put me on speaker so Mack can hear?" Burke said.

"I'm here, buddy," Mack said.

"It's good to hear your voice, Mack."

"You missed me, didn't you? I'm just glad I can help with this even if I'm sitting here in the infirmary and y'all are having all the fun in Damascus."

"No fun yet, but it's almost time to punch that clock."

"HUA," Mack said. "So what do you need from me?"

"Jonesy's trying to locate Emily with the drone as we speak. And as for the vehicles, thermal imagining told us there are at least ten individuals inside."

"*Ten*," Mack said, louder than expected.

Lily added, "Is that bad?"

"It's not good," Burke said.

"You know what that means, Burke," Mack said.

"I do."

Lily cut Burke off before he could say more. "Uh, someone want to clue me in on what we're talking about here?"

"They're there for one reason," Burke said.

Mack interrupted before Burke could finish the cold hard truth. "To kill Emily, Natasha, and Lopez once they have the drive."

"That's our take too," Burke said.

"So what are you gonna do?" Lily said.

"Well, taking out ten men in the middle of Damascus in broad daylight is going to attract a lot of attention."

Mack cut in. "A lot of negative attention from the local authorities as well as terror groups in the area."

"Yeah, that's our thinking as well," Burke said. "Which is why I need to speak with Stallone."

"Stallone? What? Why?" Lily said.

Again, before Burke could answer, Mack did instead. "Because Burke needs his permission since this could turn really ugly and be a political nightmare."

Burke smiled. "That's why I love you, Mack. It's like we share a brain."

"I didn't have to be some tactical genius to figure that out, Burke, but I appreciate the fact that you said you love me. It makes . . . makes me feel all . . . warm inside," Mack teased.

"Shut it."

Mack laughed. "Consider it shut."

Then Lily came back over the phone and said, "Do you need me to go find Stallone now?"

"I do. Do you think you can?"

"Of course, but . . ."

"But what?" Burke said.

"I'm afraid he's going to say no. Tell you to leave her there to die for the sake of self-preservation and not wanting to start a war with Syria."

"Pshh. Syria. We'd smoke 'em in a day," Burke said. "But it's their allies that could make Stallone and the president nervous. Which is why I need his approval."

"All right," Lily said. "I'll go find him."

"Thanks, Lily."

Then Burke looked over at Jones, who was staring intently at something on the drone screen.

"What is it?" Burke asked.

"It's hard to tell, but with the thermal it looks like there are two people close together—like real close. Almost in a hug. And the other is taking an offensive stance. Like . . ." Jones looked up from the screen.

Burke filled in the blank. "A standoff."

Jones nodded, and Burke pounded the dashboard.

"Can you fly lower?" Burke asked. "Switch back to the camera. See if you can see through a window or something. See if you can confirm what we see through thermal."

"Roger that," Jones said.

Burke whipped around and caught sight of Jericho and Sammy. "Be ready to move. No matter what Stallone says, we're going as soon as I hang up the phone. Just because I'm asking doesn't mean we need his permission. This is just protocol. We're not leaving Emily to die."

Both men readied their weapons and reached for their respective door handles and were ready to bust out on Burke's order.

"*Burke*." Stallone's voice boomed through the speaker. "Where are you?"

"In Damascus, sir."

"Damascus? What the hell are you doing there? You were supposed to be moving on Rajabi at zero one thirty."

"We're not outside Rajabi's compound, sir."

"Then where are you?"

"I told you—"

"Yeah, yeah, you said Damascus. But where? And why?"

Burke filled Stallone in on everything Emily had told him, including the tidbit that Lopez was still breathing. Burke then gave his side of the story and why the situation was so dire and needed immediate attention.

"And you're outside the building now?" Stallone said.

"That's right," Burke said.

"And you're sure they're in the correct building and Lopez has access to the flash drive?" Stallone said.

"We've not heard otherwise, sir."

Stallone was silent for five seconds. Jones's knees were bouncing, agitated, like he wanted to say something and was having trouble waiting. He rolled his finger and told Burke to put the phone on speaker. Burke complied.

"Sir, this is Bart Jones."

"What is it, Jones?"

"Sir, I have a visual from outside the building?"

"How?"

"Our drone."

"What do you see?"

"It looks like Lopez is holding Natasha hostage, sir. And Emily has her gun trained on him as we speak."

"What? How? How did it come to this?" Stallone said.

Burke interjected, "Sir, if I may."

"Speak, Burke. And quick!"

"The details surrounding Lopez's death, or nondeath, were strange. We're thinking—and Emily thought this, too, which is why she was prepared with the Glock—that Lopez has turned against us or somehow been forced to."

"The bastard."

"Yes, sir."

"So you think he was going to kill both women and take the flash drive to Rajabi?"

"That was our estimation, sir."

"Why?" This seemed like a question to himself. A split second later, he replied, "Put him down, Burke. Put him down hard. You understand me?"

"I do, sir. And what about the men on the street?"

"Do whatever it takes, Burke. You cannot let Rajabi get his hands on that flash drive."

"Understood, sir."

Burke hung up the phone and tossed it onto the console. He looked over at Jones and said, "Get us closer to that building, Jonesy. In fact, I don't care if you drive right through the front door. Just make it fast!"

"With pleasure." Jones shifted into drive and peeled out of the lot.

"You sure this is a good idea, Burke?" Jericho said. "Might be more tactical to come in from the opposite side. Or spread out and take the vehicles from an elevated position."

"Ordinarily, I'd agree with you, Jericho, but Emily's in trouble. No way we can risk losing her or Natasha. If Lopez shoots them both and gets out of the building, no way we could cut him off before he got picked up by his goons. We need the element of surprise on our side. So, like I said, punch it, Jonesy. And don't bother knocking before entering, if you know what I mean."

CHAPTER THIRTY-EIGHT

"No more talking," Lopez said. "Give me the flash drive."

Emily aimed her Glock at his head. She was standing less than twenty feet away. "You know I can't do that," Emily said.

"You will, or Natasha dies."

Natasha stared at Emily. Emily could see it in her eyes. Natasha was calm, not scared like most people would be. Emily watched her raise her hands to her side as if she was about to make a move, when suddenly a loud crash from beneath them echoed up to their location five stories up.

Emily shuddered at the sound and dropped the barrel of the Glock slightly. In that moment of distraction, Natasha reached up and grabbed hold of Lopez's bandaged hand. He screamed in pain, and she pushed herself out of his hold. She took two steps away from him. As he raised his gun, Emily pulled the trigger and filled his chest full of lead. With each bullet hitting its mark, Lopez was sent off balance, and on the fifth shot, he stumbled over some stacked drywall and fell hard against the pile. His gun went flying and landed on the concrete close to Natasha. She picked up the gun and aimed it at Lopez as he lay there. She squeezed the trigger three more times, but only two hit their mark. She wanted to be sure he would not be getting up.

Emily moved to Natasha's side and reached for the gun and made her lower it. "It's okay. He's gone."

Natasha bent down and reached into his pocket and lifted his phone. She looked up at Emily and explained, "So we can track Rajabi."

"Good thinking," Emily said.

More shots rang out from below. Emily's eyes went wide. *Burke?* She was so engrossed in the fight with Lopez that she didn't realize the noise from below might have been him. She ran to the front of the building and looked out the window toward the ground below. Men were spread across the street in a formation and opening fire.

"We gotta get down there and help him," Emily said. She turned around to see Natasha pointing a gun directly at her chest. Emily blinked rapidly. She couldn't believe it. "Natasha, what are you doing?"

"It's not personal, Emily," she said as she shrugged. "It's just . . . business."

Emily stepped toward her. "Ah." Natasha moved her gun closer. "Don't take one more step."

Think, Emily, think. "You know you're never going to get away with this."

"You know, you're probably right. But if I do, the possibility of millions of dollars in my bank account seems a lot more appealing than this life of a spy I'm living."

"The CIA—even your own country will hunt you down. There's nowhere you could go that we won't find you."

"Same old clichés." Natasha tossed her hand.

"Okay, how about this? You won't make it out of the building. Because as soon as Burke finds out, he won't hesitate to put a bullet in you."

"He will if you're my hostage."

Emily didn't think it would come to that.

Natasha continued, "Besides, we might be able to slip out the back door without him even knowing we're gone. He's got those bullets down there to worry about. Now move!" She waved her gun and instructed Emily to go first.

When Emily came to the staircase, she stared down and heard a familiar voice.

"*Emily*," Burke yelled. "Where are you?"

Natasha held her finger to her mouth and shook her head. Through the half-constructed staircase, she saw Burke and one other moving up to the second floor. As they disappeared from the staircase to check floor two, Natasha nodded, and Emily continued ahead slowly. If only she could stall a bit, maybe she could make the descent long enough for Burke to find her.

Her thoughts were interrupted by a sudden hard hit to the back of her head.

"Ow! What the—" When Emily whipped around, Natasha shoved the barrel of her handgun into Emily's forehead.

"Faster." Natasha's eyes narrowed.

Emily could see the seriousness on her face. She wasn't messing around. By the time they reached the fourth floor, Natasha said in a whisper, "Wait. We're hiding here." She grinned at Emily and yelled out, "*Burke*! *Burke*! Come quick, we're on the fifth floor. It's Lopez. He's got a gun on Emily."

Emily ground her teeth. She wanted to reach out and slap her to wipe the grin off her face, but if she did, she'd be dead. She thought of Burke, and wondered, if Natasha killed her, would she go after him and kill him too?

"We're coming, Emily," Burke cried out.

"Not a word," Natasha whispered. "Or I'll kill you both."

They waited and hid behind some stacked wood on the floor. They watched as Burke raced up the staircase. Emily raised up on her feet, and as she was about to speak, Natasha noticed what she was doing, then reached over and shoved her gun against Emily's temple.

After Burke climbed up to the fifth story, Natasha grabbed her arm and led her back toward the staircase. She pushed Emily forward, and they began descending the stairs, this time with a little more speed. As they continued their way down, Emily was formulating a plan, but every scenario in her mind didn't end well.

Then she thought of what Stallone had said: the flash drive meant more to the CIA than her life, V's life, or even Burke's life. Stallone was clear from the beginning. If they get V back alive, fine, but the flash drive *was* the mission, and Emily wouldn't let it go without a fight.

With only ten steps remaining until they reached the first level, Emily put some distance between herself and Natasha. Emily was two steps ahead, and as she came to the first floor, she leaped from four steps and rolled into a somersault. The move caught Natasha off guard, and once Natasha reached the floor herself, Emily jumped from the ground and sprinted directly at her. Emily put her shoulder in Natasha's midsection—a perfect form tackle just as Burke had taught her. The impact from Emily's attack knocked Natasha's gun from her hand, causing the gun to go off.

Emily moved her body quickly over Natasha's. She straddled her in mount position. As she pressed down with her hips, she put her forearm to Natasha's throat. Burke had taught her this: position first, then attack. Next she brought her right elbow back, ready to smash down on Natasha's nose. Before she could execute, however, an explosion erupted in front of the building. The force from the blast threw Emily off Natasha into a nearby wall.

The wind was sucked from her lungs, and she gasped for air. Her ears rang, and her focus was shaky. When she was able to get on all fours, she looked toward the front of the building. The SUV that Burke had run into the building was on fire. It looked like it had been shot with an RPG or some other explosive device. She saw the outline of two men crawling on all fours, searching for something on the ground, maybe their weapons.

She heard one of them speak. "Burke." It was Jones. "Get down here. The building's gonna go. We need to get the hell outta here."

Emily searched for any sign of Natasha, but she found nothing. She was gone. And the building was about to come tumbling down on everyone left inside.

CHAPTER THIRTY-NINE

THE SHOCK FROM THE RPG DIDN'T KNOCK BURKE OFF HIS FEET, but it did send a shiver up his spine. He was five stories up, and it was only a matter of time before the building would come crashing down.

"What do we do with him?" Sammy said as he hovered over Lopez's dead body.

"Leave him. There's no time." Burke stopped to look around. "Emily! Natasha!" There was no sign of either one of them. Something was wrong. He turned and looked back at Sammy. "We need to get out of here. *Now.*"

Burke sprinted down the staircase. He heard more bullets penetrating the glass and metal below. Bullets tore through the glass as they descended each floor. The men outside were shooting up every bit and piece of the building, trying to get a lucky shot on Burke or one of his men.

"*Jones*! *Emily*! Can you hear me?" Burke yelled as he ran.

Jones called out from below. "Burke, we're taking heavy fire."

"Do you have eyes on Emily?" Burke yelled.

"Yeah. I got her now. She's hurt, Burke. Took some shrapnel to the leg in the blast."

Burke was on the third-floor landing and descending fast. "Shoot the glass at the back of the building. Grab Emily, Jericho, and get the hell out of here."

Burke heard Jones shoot toward the back of the building. He was on the second-floor staircase as more bullets battered the inside of the empty space. With nothing to stop the rounds, multiple shots whizzed past Burke's ear. One rogue bullet struck him right in the meat of his left arm above the bicep.

"*Ahhh,*" Burke cried out.

"Burke, you all right?" Sammy caught up and reached for him.

"Fine. We can't stop. Just go."

Sammy jumped ahead of Burke, and once they reached the first floor, the entire building shifted. Like a house of cards, the right side swayed first. Sammy grabbed ahold of Burke, and they sprinted to their left. The open glass where Jones had shot the hole wasn't far, maybe another twelve feet, but even in that short amount of distance, Burke didn't know if the building would hold together long enough for them to get out in time.

Through the empty void, Burke saw Jones and Jericho carrying Emily outside, away from the building. They were running down the sandy hill just off the back of the building.

At least she made it, Burke thought to himself. If she survived, Burke could rest easy.

The unmistakable sound of approaching sirens grew ever closer, and the bullets ceased to exist. Burke didn't know if it mattered; the damage had been done, the building was coming down, and there was nothing he could do to stop it.

Two more steps and Burke was in the frame of empty glass. As he went to take a third step, he heard an audible pop—a crack of cables snapping—then the sound of metal collapsing on top of metal.

Burke and Sammy rushed outside before the building fell, but they needed to get far enough away from the flying debris. Their only hope was to tumble down the hill and let their momentum carry them to safety. That was good in theory, but that same hill would carry the debris field even closer as the building fell down the hill behind them.

Burke tumbled end over end, and with each crash on the hard-packed sand, a jolt of pain ran through his body. He must have rolled a hundred feet or more from the building before he finally came to a stop. As he lay there in pain, staring at the blue sky, an avalanche of concrete, brick, metal, rebar, glass, and wood came rolling toward him with nothing to stop it.

"*Burke*!" Jones call out.

But Burke couldn't move. He was stuck there, injured, at the mercy of the falling debris. As he lay there waiting for his own demise, he felt someone grab his leg. He looked up to see who was holding his boot, but the sun was blocking his face.

"I got ya, Burke." He recognized the voice. It was Jones.

Then someone else grabbed his other boot. Jericho.

"Sammy?" Burke said. "Where's Sammy? He was with me. Did he make it out?"

"He did, Burke," Jericho said. "He was just able to get out safely."

Burke breathed a sigh knowing no one else had been lost under his command. They dragged Burke further from the site. When they stopped, Burke scooted to his butt. Before he could rise to a knee, Emily lunged for him and wrapped him in a tight bear hug.

"Thank you, Burke. Thank you, for coming for me," she said.

When she pushed out of the hug, Burke said, "It was a team effort."

She looked to each man and nodded, then hugged each of them.

When Burke rose to his feet, he looked down at her leg. "Can you walk?"

"Can you?" she replied with a chuckle as she looked him up and down.

"I may look like hell, but it's gonna take a lot more than a building falling on me to take me out," he said, smiling.

She hobbled a bit. "I think I can manage."

"Where's Natasha?" Burke said.

"She bolted after the explosion."

"She turned on you too?"

"Yeah," Emily said as her shoulders slumped.

"Rough day. I'm assuming she took the flash drive?"

Emily limped as she turned to face Burke. "She did."

"We need to move," Burke said.

"We got her." Jericho and Sammy lifted Emily under her arms to help her walk.

"Good. Then let's get out of here. We'll worry about everything else once we're safe. Those sirens may have chased Rajabi's men away for now, but I don't want to get tracked down by local authorities or any more men Rajabi might be pointing toward us. We need to regroup."

"I saw a neighborhood nearby on the map before we rolled in here," Jericho said.

"You think you can guide us there?" Burke said.

"Yeah, it's just over that hill there." Jericho pointed to his right. The hill wasn't more than a quarter mile, but that was still a lot of ground to cover surrounded by potential threats.

As they started their trek, Burke looked at Jones. "How many did you take out on the street before they fired the RPG?"

"Tough to say. Three. Maybe four."

"I got three for sure," Jericho said.

"Leaving three or four still out there," Burke said.

"You think they'll circle back? Come after us?" Jones said.

"Depends on how corrupt the local government is. But I can't imagine they're going to be too excited about another firefight in the middle of a neighborhood. I don't think we worry about that now, because we need to contact Stallone."

"You think he's going to be pissed about the flash drive?" Emily said.

"I'm sure he will be, but that wasn't your fault," Burke said to reassure her.

"Natasha screwed us over for the sake of a payday. Did any of you see which way she went?" Emily asked.

They all shook their heads.

"Like I said, calling Stallone is imperative," Burke said.

"Why's that?" Jones said.

"Because once Rajabi finds out the flash drive is in Natasha's hands, V is as good as dead. If we ever want to see her alive again, Stallone needs to move in on his compound now, not zero one thirty."

CHAPTER FORTY

Rajabi was sitting at his desk, working, when a knock on the door interrupted his thoughts.

"What is it?" he said.

The man from outside the door spoke loudly. "Phone call for you, sir. A woman calling from Lopez's phone."

"A woman?" he mumbled to himself. It was rare that he spoke to any woman, especially one calling from Lopez's phone. "What does she want?"

"She says she has the flash drive and wants to speak with you."

Rajabi pushed away from his walnut desk and jogged to the door. When he swung it open, Jellel was standing there with the phone outstretched. Rajabi yanked it from his hand and turned to close the door.

"Who is this?" Rajabi got right to the point.

"Natasha Zielinski."

"Natasha . . ." Rajabi tried to place her. "You're the one watching the building."

"That's right."

Rajabi scrunched his brow. "You must have my flash drive."

"I do."

"And since you're calling from Lopez's phone, I can only assume he's dead."

"He is."

"So, what . . . you're calling me to gloat? Tell me you're going to come after me, after V? Give me some kind of cliché? Well, you can forget about that. Now that you have the flash drive, she's as good as—"

"No," she said, cutting him off.

"No what?"

"No, I'm not calling to gloat. I'm calling to make a deal."

Rajabi scrunched his brow. "A deal?"

"That's right. You still want the flash drive, correct?"

"Of course, but . . . how do I know I'm not walking into a trap? How can I trust you?"

"Because I want money. Loads of it. And if you pay me, you can kill V. I won't put up a fight."

Rajabi switched gears, and a smile grew on his face. He couldn't believe how ruthless Natasha was. He had misjudged her when he heard her speaking with Lopez. "How much do you want for it?"

"What's it worth to you?" Natasha said, testing the waters.

"I'll give you five million, US."

She laughed halfheartedly. "Not worth it. I can sell it on the open market for ten times that amount, maybe more."

"So is that your asking price then, *fifty million*?"

"Seems like a fair offer, don't you think? I mean, if the director of the CIA was willing to risk his agents in a life-or-death effort, I'd say it's more than a fair offer. After all, you wouldn't want this falling into your enemies' hands. That wouldn't turn out well, not for you or your closest allies."

Rajabi bit his lower lip. He couldn't believe he was being forced to play all his cards. Fifty million was a lot of money, but it seemed Natasha truly understood the value of the flash drive and what it meant to him.

"It's going to take some time to pull that kind of money together," Rajabi said.

"I'm not looking for suitcases full of cash here, Rajabi. You've got an hour."

"An *hour?*"

"That's right. Call your bank. Or log into an offshore account and get your money ready to transfer. I'll meet you at the *Hotel Shakar* in downtown Damascus in one hour for the exchange. But only after the money is in my account."

Before Rajabi could talk about needing more time, she had ended the call. In his anger, Rajabi chucked the phone against the wall, breaking it into tiny pieces. He yelled for Jellel outside the door, and he opened it quickly.

"Yes, sir."

He was seething. "Where's Cyrus?"

Jellel shrugged and said, "I don't know, sir."

"Find him." Rajabi stepped toward his man. "Get him on the phone. I don't care what you have to do." He was getting closer, within arm's reach. Jellel gulped, not knowing what Rajabi might do. Rajabi reached for the door and screamed, "*I need answers*." Then he slammed the door shut in Jellel's face.

Rajabi turned back into the room and saw the phone shattered and realized he needed to make another call. He needed to alert Dimitri so he could relay the information to his connection in the Iranian government.

"*Jellel*," Rajabi called out.

Jellel opened the door. He was on the phone trying to locate Cyrus. "Yes, sir."

"I need your phone."

Jellel pointed to it and said, "I'm calling Cyrus."

"Forget Cyrus. He clearly didn't do his job. He's dead anyway." He didn't know that for a fact, but Rajabi moved toward Jellel and ripped the phone from his hand and dialed Dimitri.

When Dimitri answered, in Russian he questioned who was calling.

"Saam," Rajabi said.

"Oh, Saam, how are you?" Dimitri's thick Russian accent played over the phone. "What's happened to your phone?"

He looked at his demolished phone on the floor. "Dropped it."

"How did you—" Dimitri said.

"Never mind that, I'll soon have the flash drive."

"How? Did the girl give you the location?"

"Not exactly."

"How then?"

"*How* is not important. The important thing is I'm going to be meeting someone in Damascus within the hour to make the exchange."

"Exchange with who?"

"That's too many questions, Dimitri," Rajabi said.

It's not that Rajabi didn't trust Dimitri; Rajabi just did not want the message conveyed to Iran that he had lost his nerve and somehow couldn't be trusted in future endeavors. Rajabi wanted to be playing chess, while everyone else was playing checkers.

"Sorry. Then what do you need from me?" Dimitri said.

"I need you to be ready to call your contact in the Iranian government. Be ready to tell them that when I get the flash drive in my hand, the rockets will be in the air in a matter of minutes. They need to be ready to have their story straight. I don't want it to come as a shock."

"Understood."

"Good. Thank you, Dimitri. I knew I could count on you."

"You're welcome."

"Keep your phone close, and I'll be in touch soon. There's just one thing I need to do before I leave."

"What's that?"

A wide smile grew on Rajabi's face. "It will feel so sweet to eliminate a CIA operative in my own home."

"Isn't it always sweet to kill the infidels?"

"Of course it is. But maybe more so if they're with the CIA."

Both men laughed; then Rajabi hung up and went to the door. He opened it and handed the phone back to Jellel.

"Keep that on you, and follow me."

The men walked through the compound until they reached the room where Veronica was being held. Rajabi nodded to the man standing guard, who then slipped the key inside the lock and opened the door.

Rajabi stepped into the room. The lights were bright, and the meal his men had provided for her was untouched. Veronica faced the wall.

"Get on your knees," Rajabi said.

She didn't move.

"I said, get on your knees."

Again, she stayed put. Proud. Determined. And it seemed she would not be shaken by his words. Rajabi snapped his fingers, and Jellel entered behind him. He walked over to Veronica and grabbed her from the bed and dragged her toward Rajabi. She reached up and scratched at Jellel's hand, but he was too strong and wouldn't let go.

Jellel set her down in front of Rajabi, but she refused to get on her knees. When Rajabi bent down in front of her, Veronica thrashed her hand forward and stuck him hard in the cheek with a homemade shank from the silverware provided. She growled at him and pounced from the ground, but Jellel cut off her attack and with one punch shattered her jaw.

As she lay in pain, Rajabi nodded for Jellel to finish the job while he exited the room to tend to his fresh wound. Before he left, Rajabi watched Jellel reach around Veronica's neck and give one hard snap.

CHAPTER FORTY-ONE

"BURKE? IS THAT YOU?" STALLONE YELLED THROUGH THE PHONE.

Emily, Jones, Sammy, and Jericho looked at Burke, shocked that they could hear Stallone's voice through the speaker.

"Yes, sir," Burke said.

"What happened? Are you okay? We saw the building collapse on the satellite. And some people running away as it fell."

"We're all okay, sir. Well, all of us except for Lopez."

"Lopez?" he questioned. "What happened to him? Was he able to get the flash drive?"

"Yes, sir. He and V had hidden the flash drive inside a wall on the top floor. Emily got it out."

Stallone laughed excitedly. "That's excellent news. I'm so proud of her."

"Sir," Burke said, interrupting him. It was odd that Stallone wasn't somber over losing a member of the CIA. "He'd turned on us."

"Who, Lopez?"

"Yes, sir. He was in Rajabi's pocket."

"So you all were right. He double-crossed us."

"Afraid so," Burke said. "He came to the building to blackmail Natasha and Emily. He couldn't get into the building without

Natasha's say-so. She was the one with the detonator. The building was rigged with C4 to blow."

"Right, that much we knew, correct?" Stallone said.

"We did, sir, but it turned out there was more to the story."

"What do you mean? All is well, correct? We have the flash drive?"

"No, sir. We do not."

"*Burke*!" Stallone shouted. "What are you saying?"

"I'm saying that Natasha turned on us, too, sir. She stole the flash drive from Emily and took her hostage just before the building came crashing down."

Stallone breathed heavily. "So where is Natasha now?"

"Gone, sir," Burke said.

"Gone?"

"That's right. She escaped."

An audible pop echoed in Burke's ear. Stallone must have smacked a wall or a desk. Burke took the phone away and stared at the speaker, wondering what was going to come next.

"Burke, this is unacceptable. You know how important that flash drive is."

"I know, sir, and we'll track Natasha down. Right now, though, we need to find a vehicle. And we're going to need Lily's help. But, sir, that's not the only problem."

He huffed through the phone. "It seems that's all you've been creating lately."

Burke bit his lip and checked his ego. If he lashed out at Stallone, he knew it wouldn't save V's life. He needed to play it cool. He wanted to show Stallone the softer side of him, show a side of humanity.

"I know and I'm sorry, sir, but . . ."

"But what, Burke?"

"V needs our help."

Again, Stallone sighed heavily through the phone.

Burke continued. "We need to attack Rajabi's compound now. You need to send the secondary team in, or V won't last."

"She'll do what she is trained to do."

Burke held his breath. He couldn't believe Stallone was being so callous. "Sir, you know as well as I do that once Natasha reaches out to Rajabi, V's as good as dead."

There was silence on his end.

"Sir. Did you hear me?"

"I heard you, Burke, but I'm not going to send in a rescue team and risk their lives for the sake of one agent. She knew the risks when she accepted this assignment."

"So, what, you're just going to leave her to Rajabi and his men?"

"People die in this business every day, Burke. Don't get sentimental about it. It's part of life. Part of being an agent. Her loss will be felt, and her service rewarded, but . . . I can't in good conscience risk any more lives. She might already be dead."

Burke swallowed the hard truth. Then it came to him. "She was always going to be the sacrificial lamb, wasn't she, sir?"

Stallone didn't answer. Instead, he was gone and Lily came back over the line.

"Burke, are you okay?" Lily said.

Burke dropped his head and mumbled, "I hate it when he does that."

"What was that?" Lily said.

"Never mind. I'm fine, Lily."

"Good. Glad to hear it."

"Lily, I need you to do something for me."

"Name it," she whispered.

"I need you to find Natasha. Did you see her leave?"

"To tell you the truth, Burke, it's hard to pick out any one person from the overhead satellite image, especially in that chaos. Y'all look like little ants scavenging around a hill."

"She would've gotten out of the building before the rest of us. She would've run south."

"I'll look, Burke, but I can't rewind the live satellite feed. The best I can do is try to locate her on CCTV, but . . ."

Burke knew what she was going to say. "That would be like finding a needle in a stack of needles."

"It would be difficult, yes."

Burke put his hand to his head. He had to think of the next best option. "What about Rajabi?"

"What about him?"

"Do you have eyes on his compound?"

"Of course. We have been monitoring the compound ever since you arrived at the building."

"Has there been any movement?"

"Not recently."

Burke mumbled to himself something

Lily couldn't hear. "What's that, Burke?"

"Never mind. Keep watching him. I can almost guarantee Natasha will be in touch with him. If she wants a quick payday—which she will 'cause she's gonna need a lot of cash to run and hide from us and her own government—he is the only one likely to pay and pay now."

"You think Rajabi will go to meet her?"

"I can almost guarantee it. So forget trying to locate her. Stay on him. And he'll lead us right to her."

"That's a good plan, Burke."

"Thanks, Lily. Keep me in the loop. We're trying to find a vehicle. Once we get one, I'll call back, but if you see any movement on Rajabi's end, you call me first, got it?"

"You got it."

"Oh, one more thing."

"Name it."

"If and when you see Rajabi, see if you can get eyes on V. See if for some reason they move her around the compound. Maybe take her along for the ride. The best we can hope for is, maybe Natasha offered a trade to keep her alive—maybe in exchange for the flash drive."

"You think she would have done that?" Lily's voice rose, encouraged.

"I can only hope, but . . . honestly, I don't know. As much as I hate to say it, at this point V's life is in Natasha's hands."

CHAPTER FORTY-TWO

RAJABI STARED INTO HIS BATHROOM MIRROR, WHICH WAS OUTLINED with solid gold. Normally, his servants had the gold shining, but as he washed his face, some blood splattered over the perimeter and contaminated the glossy sheen.

Rajabi reached for the wounds on his cheek and recoiled in pain. The tines of the fork-shank cut him deep—not all the way into his mouth but deep enough that he could feel the gash as he tongued inside his own cheek.

He placed some cotton balls on the counter, then took some rubbing alcohol and poured it over the cotton. He placed the ball into his hand and pressed it to his cheek. He gritted his teeth and clenched his fist as a burning sensation cut through the wound.

He lifted his fist and pounded the marble countertop. When he lifted his eyes to examine the wound, he couldn't believe he had let a woman—a Westerner—get the better of him. Even though V was now dead, he wished he could've made more of an example out of her.

As he continued to clean his wound, Jellel's phone rang on the counter next to the cotton balls. It was Dimitri.

"What is it?"

"Are you on the road?" Dimitri said.

"Not yet. Just had to take care of the girl."

"Is it done? Did you kill her?"

"I did." Even though she had left a lasting mark, he was proud of this feat.

"Good," Dimitri said. "I just wanted to give you an update. I have spoken to my contact. You have the green light to launch the rockets once you acquire the flash drive."

"Of course I do," Rajabi snapped. "As if I needed their permission."

"Relax, Saam." Dimitri could tell something had thrown him off.

Rajabi knew he had spoken out of turn. "Sorry, Dimitri. I . . . I just want the flash drive back so we can end all of this."

"You mean *start* this," Dimitri said. "Because I don't know about you, but I would love to see Jerusalem burn."

"Yes. And it will. It's only a matter of time," Rajabi said.

"The minute you get the flash drive, you need to call me, understood?"

"Consider it done." Rajabi ended the call.

He looked down at the unwrapped gauze on his countertop. He reached for it, then stopped. He wanted his face to remain the way it looked now. Maybe the unsightly scar would help make sure Natasha didn't try to swindle him once he made it to the hotel in downtown Damascus.

He stepped from his room into his closet. Dozens of finely pressed suits hung on the racks. He walked over to look at himself in the floor-to-ceiling mirror. His white shirt was bloodstained, dotted with more and more red as his cuts dripped onto it.

"Jellel!" Rajabi called over his shoulder.

His guard appeared from around the corner and said, "Yes, sir."

"How do I look?" he asked as he looked at his reflection in the mirror.

Jellel wasn't sure if the question was rhetorical. "What do you mean, sir?"

"I mean, do I look intimidating?" Rajabi spread his chest wide.

"Of course, sir."

That was good enough for him. He needed his man to stroke his ego. He had passed the test. And if Jellel thought he looked intimidating, well, then he figured, why change?

"Let's move," Rajabi said.

Rajabi led Jellel out of his bedroom and through the living area of the compound. As they walked, Rajabi glanced at his watch, making sure they would have enough time to make it to the hotel. Even though he didn't wait for many people, the last thing he needed was to be late for this meeting.

Once Rajabi walked out his front door and reached his waiting vehicle, another vehicle was coming up his driveway.

"Who's that?" Rajabi used his hand to shield his eyes from the brightness of the sun.

Jellel joined him by his side. "That looks like Cyrus. Maybe some of the others."

Rajabi took a deep breath. What would he say to his most trusted man? Rajabi watched Cyrus drive the vehicle toward the house with haste. When he came to a complete stop, Cyrus jumped out of the truck, followed by only two other men.

"Cyrus." Rajabi walked toward him and reached out his arms, pretending to be happy to see him. "How are you?"

"Sir, we came as fast as we could," Cyrus said, bowing his head. "The building, sir. We took it down."

"What do you mean you took the building down?" Rajabi didn't know all the details surrounding the firefight.

"We couldn't get inside to get Lopez and the girl. So we brought the building down on top of them. And now no one will ever be able to get the flash drive." Cyrus turned his nose up, almost as if proud of this failure turned success.

Rajabi looked toward the ground and laughed. The other men joined in the laughter because they were afraid of what Rajabi might do to them if they did not.

"Do you know for a fact no one got out alive?" Rajabi asked.

"No way anyone could survive a building falling on top of them, sir."

Rajabi leaned in close so only Cyrus could hear, and he whispered, "But someone did survive, Cyrus. And they have my flash drive."

Before Cyrus could attempt to defend himself, Rajabi flipped open a blade in his pocket and cut across Cyrus's throat.

Cyrus grabbed the gash and flailed with the opposite arm. He did his best to stop the inevitable, but as he reached for his neck, he gasped for air that wasn't coming. When Cyrus finally succumbed, he fell at Rajabi's feet, who stood above him and watched.

Rajabi turned to Jellel. "Don't bother picking him up. We're never coming back here. In fact, before we leave, burn it—burn it all to the ground."

"What about all the valuables inside the home, sir?" Jellel said.

Rajabi stopped and spun around one last time. "Leave it. Let it all burn with the house. More treasure awaits me in this life and the next."

CHAPTER FORTY-THREE

THE HOT SUN CAUSED BURKE TO SWEAT. THE DRIPS FROM HIS forehead fell into his eyes and made them burn. He rubbed them out as he and his team hiked across the sea of dirt and rock. Soon a roadway appeared beneath them. Burke followed the road with his eyes, and no more than a half mile down were more buildings like the ones they'd seen in the Al-Mazza Municipality.

"What are your thoughts here, Burke?" Jones said as they stopped at the top of a hill.

"We head that way." Burke nodded toward the city. "There's got to be a vehicle we can get our hands on."

"You mean, one that we can steal?" Emily said.

"If it comes to that, yes. But I like to use the term *borrow*," Burke said.

Emily laughed. "Of course you do, Burke. I've seen you 'borrow' many vehicles in our short time together." She had her fingers in air quotes.

"But I always bring them back," Burke said, trying to save face.

"You do *not*," Emily snapped back. "You must have bumped your head falling out of that building 'cause I know you remember the trucks, cars, and boats you never returned in Nigeria."

"Well, yeah, but that was in the name of freedom," Burke teased. "And in the name of saving you."

"It's always in the name of freedom, brother," Jericho said with a laugh. "At least that's what I tell my superiors."

They moved down the hill toward the road as quickly as they could, but they were hampered due to their injuries. Jones had been able to stop the bleeding in Burke's arm, but he couldn't get the bullet out. Jones also cleaned Emily's wound best he could, but she still needed medical attention to avoid infection. Bottom line, they were thirsty and hungry, and they were five lost Westerners in the middle of a hostile country with a little more than fifty rounds of ammunition among them and no clue where to go next.

As they walked, Burke's mind wandered back to his wife, Laura, and how much he enjoyed the way their relationship had been going since he'd saved her from Senator Wainwright. Who knew it would take a kidnapping—and then Burke's subsequent rescue—to rekindle the flame in their marriage that had been suppressed by anxiety and depression over their son's death.

Over the previous months, Burke had lost his taste for bourbon as well. Well, not completely, but at least he had his drinking under control. No more going to the liquor cabinet at all hours of the day to satisfy his fix. The demons he found in the bottle seemed to loosen their grip and fade away. Laura had attributed that to his newfound faith, and she had always said that sanctification takes time. This was something Burke was continuing to work through, because even with his recent transformation, he still felt the same. Still struggled with the same things he always had, but now during those struggles he was able to let them go more quickly. Give them over to God.

"*Burke*." Jones tapped him on the shoulder.

He shook his thoughts away and stared at his friend blankly.

"Everything all right in there?" He knocked on his head. "It's not wooden, is it?"

"No. Knock it off." He pushed Jones's hand away.

"You sure about that?" Jones said. "'Cause your phone's been ringing nonstop and you're not picking it up."

Burke looked at his phone; Lily was trying to call him back. "Lily, oh, hey, did you find her?"

"Um, do you mean V or . . ." She wanted him to fill in the blank.

"Yeah, V."

"No, Burke, I didn't see her exit Rajabi's compound. Rajabi's gone, and I'm tracking him now. He's headed south. Toward Damascus. Are you close?"

"We're walking toward some buildings. We'll have to steal a car once we're there, unless some Syrian citizen feels like they want to help some random rifle-toting Westerners. Which is unlikely."

"I agree with that."

"How far is his compound from Damascus?" Burke said.

"A little less than an hour."

"And you know he'll stop in the city? Or are you just speculating?"

"At this point there isn't a lot we know. I was unable to locate Natasha. She disappeared somewhere inside the city, and I don't know if she stole a vehicle herself and drove out of town or if she's in a building hiding somewhere."

"She's here. I know she is. I can almost guarantee she's been in contact with Rajabi to make a deal and he's coming to the city to collect the flash drive."

"How can you be so sure?" Lily said.

"Because it's what I'd do. I wouldn't risk crossing the border with it. I'd want to dump it off to the highest bidder. And we know Rajabi is searching for it and was willing to kill for it, so I imagine he's willing to pay for it as well. At least that's the way I would think if I were in Natasha's shoes."

"Sounds like you know a lot about how the enemy thinks, Burke."

"I just know people. Trust me. Now more than ever, I'm seeing people for what they truly are. Monsters. Nearly every one of us, especially when our backs are against the wall."

"I just can't believe she would do this if it meant something happening to V."

"I can." But then there was silence on Lily's end. Did she have more to say about V? "What is it?" Burke decided to ask.

"Before Rajabi left his compound, he lit it on fire."

Burke stopped walking.

"What is it?" Jones could tell by Burke's blank facial expression that something had happened.

"He lit it on fire?" Burke said.

His words stopped everyone else in their tracks.

"His compound is burning as we speak. I can't tell how high the flames are at this point, but there's a lot of black smoke, and by the looks of it, everything will be destroyed."

Burke gulped knowing exactly what that meant for V. She was either dead or soon to be burned alive by the flames. He held his tongue; there was nothing he could say. In his mind, the mission had always been about getting her back alive. Even if they were able to retrieve the flash drive, Burke would always consider the mission a failure without bringing her home safe.

CHAPTER FORTY-FOUR

"BURKE, DO YOU COPY?" JERICHO SAID.

Burke and the others were inside another municipality. He stood watch from the corner of a building. Emily was with him, never more than a few feet from Burke's hip, especially now that she was injured. Sammy was on the opposite end of the building, acting as another lookout while Jericho and Jones tracked down a vehicle. Jones could hotwire almost any vehicle, and he was a wiz with electronics.

"I copy," Burke said. "Loud and clear, Jericho."

"Jones has his eye on an SUV. Looks big enough for all of us to fit inside—even with room in the back for Emily to spread out."

"That sounds perfect. Can you take it?" Burke said.

"Negative?" Jericho said.

"Why not?"

"Because a woman is taking her kids out of the vehicle as we speak. Looks like she has a few bags of groceries to grab as well."

Burke nodded to himself, taking the story in. "Do not take the SUV while kids are inside. I repeat, do not take the vehicle with kids around. Do you copy?"

"I read you, Burke," Jones said over the radio. "We'll wait until she's completely gone."

"Roger that, Jonesy," Burke said. Then he eyed Emily who rested on the ground next to him and smiled.

"How often do you think about Nigeria or Cameroon?" she asked, changing the subject.

Burke shrugged. "Which parts?"

Emily stared up at him and tears formed in the bottoms of her eyes. "It's the kids for me."

Burke nodded. He understood exactly what she was going through. "Yeah, I think about them a lot too. I usually don't get sad about them, though, because I know we were able to save some of them from a hellish existence. And we took down a lot of bad men involved in the trafficking ring throughout Western Africa."

"Sure, we did. But Burke . . . you know that once we killed one, two, three, even four more will have sprouted up in their place like a Hydra."

Burke was taken aback.

She peered up at him. "What? Didn't think I knew my Greek mythology?" She tilted her head to the side. "I'll have you know I'm very well-read."

"Sure thing . . . nerd." Burke grinned and turned back to the parking lot to watch Jones and Jericho.

She scowled at him but had nothing to come back with.

Jones came back over the comms. "Burke, she's gone back inside with the kids. Do I have the green light?"

"Are there others around?" Burke strained to see for himself.

"Negative," Jericho said. "No sign of movement."

"Sammy? You see anything?" Burke said.

Sammy spoke up. "Negative. All good on my side."

"Take it down," Burke said. "But be quiet about it. Understand?"

"Roger that, Burke," Jones said.

Emily climbed to her feet and leaned next to Burke on the side of the building as both peered out. Jones and Jericho were far enough away that neither Burke nor Emily could see exactly what they were doing as they came upon the SUV.

"Do you think Jonesy will be able to get that thing started?" Emily said.

"I have no doubt. I've seen it happen many times before."

"What about the alarm?" Emily said.

Just as she spoke, the alarm echoed as it honked the SUV's horn.

Burke perked up and stood a little taller and gripped tight to his rifle. Emily grabbed hold of his arm and went rigid, but the alarm cut off after only three honks of the horn.

"See. He's got this," Burke said and gave her a pat on the shoulder to help calm her nerves. Truth was, he didn't know for sure. Stealing a car in the middle of the day in a hostile city was no easy task.

To their left, two people were walking down the sidewalk, directly toward Jericho and Jones.

Burke spoke to his earpiece. "Jericho. Get inside the SUV. You've got two civilians walking your way. They'll see you in less than five . . . four . . ." Burke trailed off.

He changed his sight line to Jericho, who opened the back door of the SUV and jumped inside. He shut the door just in time. The two people walking down the street looked toward the SUV as soon as they heard the door slam.

Burke's eyes grew big as he looked at Emily.

"That was close," Burke said.

"Too close," Jericho added through his comms.

"How much longer we got, Jonesy?" Burke said.

"Shouldn't be more than another minute." Jones's voice was strained.

Burke breathed a sigh, but his relief was cut short.

"Uh, Jonesy," Jericho said.

Burke held his breath. He couldn't see what Jericho saw.

"We don't have a minute." Jericho said. "The woman who owns the SUV is coming back outside. She'll be on top of us in ten seconds. Burke, do I have permission to engage."

"What? Are you crazy?" Burke said. "Negative. You do not have permission to engage."

"Five seconds, Burke, and we won't have a choice," Jericho said. "We gotta do something."

"Do not engage!" Burke could not have been clearer.

Then there were two seconds of silence, which seemed like a lifetime. "I got it," Jones barked.

Burke heard the squealing tires and stepped out from around the corner of the building to see the owner screaming curses in a language he didn't understand. He grabbed Emily and helped her walk as Jones pulled up next to the building. As he loaded Emily inside the back hatch, Sammy ran in from behind and jumped inside the open door.

Burke glanced back toward the screaming woman. She was chasing down her car, and she was gaining ground. Before Burke got inside, he looked at Emily. "Probably not returning this one either."

Emily laughed as she shook her head. Burke smiled as he closed the hatch; then he opened the back door and jumped inside. Jones drove forward, and they were on their way.

"Where am I headed, Burke?" Jones said.

"Just drive toward Damascus. Let me reach out to Lily. She had eyes on Rajabi last we spoke."

He reached for his phone and dialed her.

"Burke, I see him. He's in Damascus as we speak. Looks like he's staying in town. Just like you thought."

"I told ya, kid—sorry, *Lily*," Burke said.

"It's all right, I was just giving you a hard time about calling me kid. I actually don't mind it."

"Well, all right then."

"As long as I can call you Boomer."

Burke laughed. "Sure thing, kid, whatever floats your boat."

"Okay then." Lily laughed. "Now that I have a nickname, I feel like I'm officially part of the team."

"Whatever you say—so where's Rajabi?"

"Hold on . . . let me see," she said. She was trying to follow Rajabi's every move.

"Looks like he's slowing down at some kind of . . . yeah, I see it, Burke. He's at a hotel. *Hotel Shakar*. Is Jones driving?"

"He is," Burke said.

"I'll drop a pin and text it to him so he'll have the exact location."

"Perfect."

"Burke, you be careful," Lily said. "That hotel is in the middle of downtown. Lots of people. And I mean lots of them. None of whom are going to be friendly."

"I hear you." Burke's tone turned serious. "Tell Stallone the next call he gets will be from one of two people . . ." Burke paused. "Me telling him I have the flash drive . . . or the president of the United States telling him to prepare for World War Three."

CHAPTER FORTY-FIVE

RAJABI STEPPED OUT OF HIS VEHICLE AND WALKED TOWARD THE front door of *Hotel Shakar*. He looked up at the high rise and counted the number of floors, which he often did with hotels. There were fifteen. The exterior façade was constructed with marble and resembled the exterior of his own home—the one he had just torched.

The doorman nodded upon his approach. Rajabi didn't say a word to him or even acknowledge he was there to hold the door open.

Once inside, Rajabi took in the lobby. It was a two-story grand entrance with marble pillars from floor to ceiling. In the center of the hotel were two grand staircases constructed in a crescent moon style that met on the second level.

Beyond the staircase Rajabi saw an outdoor seating area off the back of the hotel lobby, featuring several circular tables with umbrellas to shade the tables from the high sun. A woman was seated at one of the tables. She stared back at him and offered a wave. He could only assume it was Natasha.

He narrowed his eyes and looked around the lobby once more to see if he saw any man or woman who looked out of place or like they could possibly be working with Natasha. After all, the last thing Rajabi wanted to do was walk into a trap.

Jellel came in from behind him and leaned into his ear. "We have two men on each side of the building. No one is getting in or out without our say-so."

"Good," he replied over his shoulder. "Stay here. If you see anyone who looks suspicious, do not hesitate to kill them. If all the people look okay, wait for my signal that we talked about in the car."

"Understood, sir," Jellel said.

Rajabi broke away from his man and started walking toward the outdoor patio. As he approached the hostess stand, the woman behind the counter asked if she could help seat him. He simply pointed to the patio and walked toward the door.

When he reached the door, he stretched out his arm and pushed it open. As he walked, he noticed two other parties sitting close by, both of whom saw him and immediately went rigid and did their best to avoid eye contact. But he paid them no mind.

As Rajabi approached, Natasha remained seated and watched his every move. He stood next to her. Too close for comfort for most people.

Natasha extended her hand and offered him a seat. "Please." Rajabi pulled out the wooden chair. He sat on the soft cushion and put his elbows on the table. "You look a lot different in person."

Rajabi interrupted her and cut right to the chase. "Where's the flash drive?"

She patted her pocket, then leaned in close and whispered, "Where's the money?"

He sat back against his chair more relaxed—now he knew he wouldn't have to play more games to chase down the flash drive.

He studied her from his seat. Then he lifted his hand and pointed at her. "You know, there's a question I wanted to ask you before this transaction takes place. Why did you decide to betray your country and call me?"

Natasha leaned her head to the side. She was not expecting this question. She hadn't expected the conversation would turn personal.

Rajabi shrugged and went on. "I mean, Lopez was an easy target. All I had to do was threaten his family, but you . . . I didn't even know about you. You were a surprise. So why did you double-cross him? You could've just as easily given the flash drive over to the CIA. Or stolen it from the CIA and let your own country reap the rewards of recovering it, so why?"

She didn't hesitate. "Money."

"Ah. So greed is your sin. You know, overabundance is not a healthy living."

"Says you." She wasn't about to be lectured by a known terrorist.

He grinned at her comeback.

"Call it greed if you want, but I like money," Natasha said. "And I know you have access to millions. I knew this was my chance to get out from my under my country's thumb. To get out on my own to start a new life."

Rajabi's curiosity had been satisfied. He was ready to be done with her. "Take out your phone."

She reached into her pocket for her phone, then placed it on the table.

"I'll need your banking information," Rajabi said. She gave it to him, and he plugged the numbers into his own phone. Then he looked back at her. "I'll need proof you have the flash drive before I transfer funds."

"Before I do that, just know that if you try anything, I'll have my man take you out. He's got a gun on you as we speak."

Rajabi leaned back against the chair and studied her. Then he looked around the area. Was she telling the truth? If there was another man, Jellel would've found him and alerted Rajabi or taken him out. Rajabi questioned the validity of her story, and every scenario he came up with in his mind led him to the same conclusion. She was lying. There was no one else.

He nodded and said, "You have my word."

She reached into her opposite pocket, pulled out the flash drive, and laid it on the table.

He eyed the small drive and recognized it immediately. A silver case with a purple mark across the top. Precisely the one that was stolen from him. There was no need to check its contents. He tilted his head to the side, and before he pushed the transfer button on his phone, he asked her another question. "Do you know what kind of palm tree that is behind you? Or its significance to Syria?"

Natasha narrowed her eyes. "Palm tree?"

"Yeah." He nodded and suggested she turn around.

She didn't know if she was being tricked, so she lifted the flash drive from the table and put it in her hand, then turned over her shoulder to see what Rajabi was alluding to. And just as she did, a bullet punctured the glass from inside the lobby and whizzed over Rajabi's shoulder and struck Natasha in the back of the head.

In one action, she tumbled to the floor in a pile. The remaining restaurant guests stared at the scene. A woman screamed once she recognized what had happened. Each man and woman jumped from their table and disappeared back into the hotel.

Rajabi rose from his seat and walked toward Natasha as she lay motionless. He bent down to roll her over. When she faced him, there was a hole through the middle of her head from the exit wound. He recoiled, then curled and bit his lower lip. "You were lying about the gunman, weren't you?" He looked around, and no one was there. "I figured as much."

Rajabi reached for her hand. He opened it and took the flash drive. Then he stood tall and looked beyond her, toward the palm tree. "It's a date palm," he said, then walked over to the tree and plucked one of the orange fruits and ate it like it was any normal day in downtown Damascus.

CHAPTER FORTY-SIX

"We're coming up on the hotel entrance now," Jones said, pointing through the windshield. "There."

Burke couldn't believe his eyes. It was Rajabi, and he was just walking out of the hotel lobby alone. Natasha was nowhere to be found.

"This could get messy," Burke said as he pulled back the charging handle on his M4. He heard the others readying their weapons. "But look before you shoot. I don't want any civilian casualties, you understand me?"

"That could be tough, Burke," Jericho said.

Burke whipped around and gave him a stern look. "None."

Jericho nodded. "Copy that."

Jones sped toward the entrance just as Rajabi's vehicle was pulling up. Burke rolled down his window and sent a three-shot burst into the front of Rajabi's car and incapacitated it. The loud blast caused alarm, and every civilian nearby screamed and either hit the ground or ran for cover.

Rajabi froze for a split second, then reached for the car door, but the door was locked. When he realized he couldn't get in, he turned and sprinted back into the hotel lobby among the panicked people.

The driver—a colossal man—jumped out of the driver's seat and opened fire on Burke's SUV. Once Jones stopped the car, Burke used the door as a shield to protect himself and opened fire on him—as did Sammy and Jericho.

Burke and the others filled the driver with multiple shots, and eventually he dropped to his knees before succumbing to the injuries and falling hard onto his face.

"Find Rajabi," Burke yelled to the others. "Emily, stay here. You're already hurt."

All four men left the SUV behind and gave chase. Burke watched the mass of people inside the lobby scattering like ants under a magnifying glass. He saw a man who looked like Rajabi sprinting up the staircase.

Burke and his men split into two-man teams. Burke and Sammy took the staircase up to the second level, while Jones and Jericho stayed on the first level to clear the area.

"Contact. Three o'clock," Jericho called over the radio.

Burke heard muzzle fire from beneath him. There was a glass balcony, but he couldn't see directly beneath it.

"One down," Jericho said.

"There's more," Jones yelled. "Behind you, Jericho, look *out*!"

Burke couldn't see what was happening downstairs. He wished he could offer backup, but he couldn't be in two places at once, and he knew Rajabi was upstairs.

As he walked along the corridor, Burke peered over the balcony and saw the outdoor patio below. People seemed to be congregating around something on the ground. Maybe a person, he couldn't tell. Burke persisted down the hallway and came to a doorway marked with a sign that had the words written in Arabic, but it also had the English spelling for "Pool."

Burke leaned to his right so he could see through the the small window in the door to the pool area, which looked empty. Strange for that time of day, especially since the pool area looked quite enticing. There was floor-to-ceiling glass that let in a ton of natural light. Burke leaned in closer and saw the sun shining through a carved ornate glass hole in the ceiling.

"Stay here," Burke said to Sammy. "Make sure Rajabi doesn't double back."

Sammy reached out for Burke's shoulder and squeezed. "You sure that's a good idea? What if he's inside."

"If he's there, I'll call for backup."

Sammy nodded.

Burke reached for the handle of the door, and to his surprise, it clicked open. When he stepped inside the pool area, it was even more beautiful than he'd witnessed from outside the door. He looked up at the glass ceiling at least twenty feet above him. There was a second level as well. Burke couldn't tell how to reach the second level of the pool area, but it did look like there were poolside rooms above. The floors and the pillars that held up the second floor were patterned marble with gold flake. And the pool itself was no ordinary rectangle; it was cut into a lagoon style.

Burke moved through the area swiftly, and he still considered it strange that no one was relaxing on the lounge chairs or comfortable couches. At the end of the pool deck there was some sort of room. He walked over to take a closer look, and he soon recognized the wide cedar door of a sauna.

As Burke grabbed the wood handle, Jones called out, "Jericho is down. And we're in a tight spot. Taking more fire. Burke, you copy?"

Burke reached for his ear, but he didn't speak. He did not want to give away his location if someone was close, but his friend was in trouble. "Sammy," Burke whispered, "leave the pool door. Go help Jones and Jericho."

"Copy that," Sammy said.

Burke pulled the sauna door open, and the wood creaked. Burke winced at the noise because he knew if Rajabi was close, it would've alerted him to Burke's position.

Burke pushed the door open as far as it would go, then stepped inside. It was a large sauna with double-decker benches. And it was very hot, the steam rising from the rocks. Burke began to sweat from the heat, and as he turned back to the door, he heard someone enter the pool area.

He ran toward the noise, and as he exited the sauna, he saw a young twenty-something wearing a bikini and headphones and staring at her phone. She was lost in her own world with no idea what was happening inside the hotel.

Burke raised his hand and waved, but she didn't see him. This distraction allowed Rajabi to slip in behind Burke. Rajabi hit Burke hard on the back of the head with the wood bucket from the sauna. The wood shards went flying, and Burke stumbled to the marble floor as his gun slid into the pool.

The woman saw the fight, screamed, then ran out the door. Rajabi didn't stop after the initial blow; he reared back and kicked Burke hard in the ribs, doubling him over. Then he picked up a nearby planter and threw it down hard on Burke's face. The ceramic pot split open upon contact, and dirt poured into his eyes and open mouth. Burke blinked feverishly trying to get the dirt out of his eyes, but he couldn't recover before Rajabi grabbed his arms and pulled him toward the water.

Burke yanked hard against Rajabi, but he was strong, stronger than Burke expected. Burke still couldn't see clearly. In the water at the edge of the pool, Rajabi got on top of Burke's back and forced him down face-first. The water washed the dirt from Burke's eyes, but being able to see again wouldn't help him escape being held underwater.

He flailed his arms to reach for the side of the pool—something that he could grab onto to prop himself up, but there was nothing.

Rajabi held him there for several seconds. Burke calmed himself. Rajabi may have been strong, but he wasn't a trained soldier. Burke relaxed, found his footing, and reared back, exploding out of the water. Rajabi tried to hold on, but the water made Burke too slick. He faltered back a couple of feet. Burke squared up and charged like a bull.

What Burke wasn't prepared for was how slippery the floor of the pool was under the rubber of his boot. He lost his footing, and Rajabi took advantage. As Burke tried to steady himself, Rajabi pulled him back toward the edge of the pool. Burke slid again in the water, and Rajabi was able to pull down on his neck at the same time. Burke's head bounced off the concrete edge and purple sparks lit up in front of his eyes. He was teetering on unconsciousness but managed to pull in a quick breath when he felt Rajabi pulling him underwater.

Everything went quiet. Burke's eyes were closed, and he watched as the purple sparks turned into spiraling streaks. He could feel Rajabi holding him under, but it didn't feel violent. It was if Burke was drifting off into nothingness. The weight of the world floated away on the waves of the water. His lungs were burning. His body was telling him to give in, but his mind had a different plan.

Burke wasn't sure if he'd actually opened his eyes, but there in the pool in front of him, he saw his son. He wasn't drowning. He looked happy playing under the water. It had been so long since Burke had seen him. Burke tried to swim toward him, but he didn't move. His son waved at him from about ten feet away.

Suddenly, the pool water around his son began to darken. Burke tried to shout. He tried to get AJ's attention, but nothing worked. The darkness closed in completely. Just like that, AJ was gone. So was the burning in his lungs. Then, inches from Burke's face, AJ reappeared. His son's eyes were wide.

Then AJ shouted, "*Wake up*!"

Burke's eyes shot open, and the bottom of the pool came into view. His lungs were out of air, but the shot of adrenaline he'd gotten from the vision of his dead son brought him enough life to fight back.

Burke took Rajabi's wrist that was holding his head underwater and peeled it back from his hair. He turned into Rajabi as he pushed off the pool floor with his feet. His head shot out of the water, and as he sucked in a breath, he wrapped his hands around Rajabi's neck. He continued breathing hard as he squeezed. Burke had always been a powerful man, but there was something extra tightening his grip. Something only a parent who'd lost their child could understand. It was rage. Not just the rage from a man trying to kill him, but even more fury from the pent-up emotion of not being able to save his son. Burke had never had anywhere to put that emotion. So now he applied it to his enemy. So much so that he felt Rajabi's Adam's apple pop in his crushing grip. His body stopped thrashing in the water.

Rajabi was dead.

Just as Burke let go, he heard the unmistakable sound of a pistol slide being racked. To his left one of Rajabi's men had him dead to rights. Burke closed his eyes and gunshots echoed throughout the pool area, but Burke didn't feel the sting of a bullet.

"Burke?" a woman's voice sounded.

Burke opened his eyes and saw the man who had been holding the gun on him was now lying facedown in a pool of his own blood. Burke turned toward the pool entrance, where Emily stood with blood running down the outside of her leg and her pistol still extended.

She had saved his life.

Burke coughed violently as he waded over to the stairs. His lungs were still full of water. Emily limped over and helped him stay upright as he exited the pool. He was exhausted. They both lowered themselves onto their backside beside the pool. Burke wanted to say something, but he couldn't stop coughing. Emily patted him on the back.

"That's it, big fella, get all that water out."

Burke coughed the remaining water out of his lungs and took a couple of much-needed breaths. He looked over at Emily. "What the —how did you?"

"How did I what? Come to rescue you?" She grinned. "Not without some difficulty, but when I heard Sammy leave you alone at the pool door, there was no way I was staying in that SUV."

"What about your leg?" Burke said with another cough.

"Well, it still hurts, and I may not have been fast, but I still made it in time." She patted him on the back some more. "What was that saying you used back in Utah? Something about how you've gotta be comfortable in uncomfortable situations?"

Burke's laugh came out as a cough, so instead of using his words, he wrapped her in a hug. After a few seconds he pulled back and smiled. "I knew you'd get it . . . eventually." Then he winked and patted her gently on the cheek. "Thank you. You saved my life."

"I guess you can subtract one off the list then. I'd say I still have four or five left to go."

Burke looked at Emily, then to Rajabi's body floating in the pool. "The flash drive."

The two of them scooted over to the edge of the pool, and together they pulled Rajabi's lifeless body onto the pool deck. Emily searched his pockets as Burke continued to regain his wits. After a bit of digging, Emily pulled her hand from one of Rajabi's pockets and smiled. She held up the flash drive for Burke to see.

"Thank goodness it's in a case." She grinned. "All that fuss for such a little thing." Her smile faded as she held her hand to her ear.

"What is it?" Burke couldn't hear because his earpiece had popped out in the pool.

Emily took out the earpiece and handed it to Burke.

"Burke, you copy?" Jones said.

"I'm here, Jonesy."

"You okay up there?"

"Barely. How 'bout you?"

"All good. But . . . Jericho is dead."

Burke's head dropped. He'd lost another man.

Jones spoke again. "That's not all, though. I think you should get down here and see this."

CHAPTER FORTY-SEVEN

BURKE AND EMILY HELPED EACH OTHER TOWARD THE TOP OF THE wide staircase; the lobby below was mostly empty. Almost everyone had left the carnage behind, and it was only a matter of time before the local authorities would have the building locked down and surrounded. But things in that part of the world seemed to take more time, especially when someone like Rajabi was involved.

Jones waited at the bottom of the staircase, and Burke called out, "It's good to see you, buddy."

"It's good to be seen." Jones shifted in place; something was weighing on him. "I really shouldn't be standing here, if you know what I mean. Jericho took a bullet for me."

Burke swallowed hard. "Where is he?"

"He's in the SUV out front. Sammy and I got him inside. Sammy's staying with him now."

Burke nodded, and once they reached the first floor, he said, "What was it that you wanted to show me?"

"First things first. Follow me." Jones waved them toward the back of the lobby.

Burke walked slowly so Emily could keep up. Jones held the door for both of them, and once Burke stepped outside, he noticed the beautiful flora and fauna surrounding the outdoor patio area. The thought that Laura would like it here crossed his mind. Dozens of palm fronds hung over the decking, and there was a wide array of red and yellow flowers.

"She's just over here." Jones stepped in front of Burke to show him the way.

Before Burke could ask who, he saw a woman lying on the ground. He knew immediately.

"Natasha," Burke said as Jones stopped next to her dead body.

Emily walked toward Jones, and Burke followed close behind. Burke bent down next to the body, rolled her head to the side, and saw the bullet wound. He noticed it had entered from the back. He pictured himself at the table. Put himself in her place and looked over his shoulder toward the palm trees. He wondered why she turned away from the glass. What caught her attention when the bullet came.

"She didn't even see it coming." Burke peered up at Jones.

"That's what I came up with too," Jones said.

Burke stood from his crouch and looked through the glass and back toward the lobby. He saw the hole that the bullet had made, and he moved toward the glass and ran his finger along the spider cracks.

"That's not all, Burke." Jones stood behind him, then put his own phone on Burke's shoulder.

"What's this?" Burke reached for the phone and grabbed it.

"Just listen."

Burke gave him a sideways glance, then put the phone to his ear.

"Jones. Get this message to Burke ASAP." It was Stallone. He wondered why Stallone hadn't called him. He felt for his own phone. It was in his pocket on his chest. He reached for it and pulled it out. It was black. Dead from the water damage. "There's been an attack on Israel. Rockets sent into Jerusalem. No one is sure whether they are the VX rockets Rajabi had planned to set off, but the city is burning as we speak. I'm hoping you were able to recover the flash drive and you have Rajabi in custody. Call me back as soon as you have him or the drive." Then Stallone was gone.

Burke stared at Jones. He went ghost white.

Emily could sense something was wrong. "What is it?"

"It's Jerusalem. It's been bombed."

Emily held her breath. "What? How? Was it Rajabi?"

Burke needed to sit. Gather his thoughts. Was it Rajabi? How did he do it? Did he set them off remotely once he got the drive from Natasha? So many questions swirled in his mind as sirens echoed in the distance.

Jones reached for Burke's arm before he could sit. "We don't have time to ponder this now, Burke—we need to move."

Burke nodded but felt liked he was having an out-of-body experience. Mindlessly he followed Jones out of the patio area and back toward the front door of the lobby. Upon their exit, Sammy drove the SUV parallel to their position so they could make a quick exit.

"*Burke*," Sammy yelled. "Get in."

Burke was shaken from his trance and heard the sirens growing louder. As soon as Emily took her place in the backseat, Burke fell onto the hard leather, and Sammy sped out of the area and drove away from the scene.

As they drove, five cars with sirens raced past them in a blur. Everyone inside turned to make sure they weren't going to be followed. Not one of the cars made a U-turn. Burke breathed a sigh of relief. They were in the clear—for now.

He looked down at his hand: he still had Jones's phone. Without thinking about what he would say, he called Stallone back.

Stallone picked up on the first ring. "Burke, that you?"

"Yes, sir."

"Tell me you have the flash drive."

"We do, sir."

There was a pause on Stallone's end, like he was celebrating, and his excitement came out with his next words. "That's amazing news. And Rajabi?"

"He's dead, sir."

More cheering came from the other end. "Burke, I owe you and your team a huge debt of gratitude."

"Yes, sir. But like you said in the message, sir, Israel was still bombed . . ." Burke paused. "How many people have died?"

Stallone's tone turned somber. "We won't know that for quite a while. But we do know who was responsible."

"Who?"

"Iran."

"Iran?" Burke was confused.

"That's right. They've taken credit for the bombing."

"So it wasn't Rajabi? The rockets didn't come from his missile silo?"

"It doesn't appear so," Stallone said. "At least not at this point, but we're still trying to narrow everything down."

"That doesn't make sense, sir. It was the Iranians. They wanted to join the war—why?"

"Them. And perhaps Russia."

"Russia? Why would Russia want to get involved in this conflict?"

"They've been strategic allies for decades. But lately there's been some chatter about a deeper alliance being formed. And perhaps with Iran entering the war, this is exactly the coming-out party Russia was looking for."

Burke swallowed hard. He knew what to say next, but he choked on his words, like he didn't want to say them. "So what are we talking about here, sir?"

"A global war, Burke. On an epic scale."

Burke paused to take in what Stallone had just told him, but he needed more answers about what had happened over the past few days.

"So attacking Rajabi was all for naught?"

"Not necessarily, Burke. You tracked down the flash drive, which was always our number one priority."

"That part you made very clear from the outset, sir. Even over V's life." Burke turned angry. "Speaking of, did you even see the fire at Rajabi's compound? I'm sure you know what happened to her?"

"Lily showed me. And I'm sorry for her loss, Burke. And as you said, the flash drive was of utmost importance."

"Why? What is on it?" Burke wanted him to say it out loud. Maybe he could hold it against him at a later date.

"Names, Burke. V wasn't clear on all the names she had found, but she was almost certain Rajabi had a list of all CIA assets. Your name,

Burke. And Laura's." That got his attention. That was the first time Stallone had included his wife's name. "Even your son's name—God rest his soul. Along with every other agent serving with an acronym in our country. At the beginning of the mission, we didn't have all the details, which is why I was being vague. It wasn't that I was trying to hide it from you, Burke; we just didn't know. Lily was able to hack into Rajabi's computer. Somehow, he got the access he needed and saved the information on that drive, which is why we needed to recover it so badly. Yes, deep down I knew V's life would likely be forfeited. Which is why she went to such great lengths to protect the sanctity of the location. Even she didn't know who she could trust. And in the end, she couldn't even trust the two people closest to her. Which is why I think she reached out to Emily in the first place."

Burke looked over at Emily. She smiled at him. He smiled back.

"I say all that to say this, Burke," Stallone said. "When you get back here, I don't want you getting too comfortable, because I—no, the world—is gonna need your team to track down the people responsible for attacking Israel."

Burke went silent for a moment. He looked at both Jones and Sammy. Then Emily next to him and Jericho dead in the back. He had lost a lot on this mission. Then he thought of Bear. Then Mack in the infirmary.

Friends closest to him were getting hurt. Some dying. But they were only the first ones to go in a war driven by so much hate and blood lust. Burke didn't start this war. And he didn't know if he could finish it, but he was going to give it everything he had to protect those who couldn't protect themselves.

"So, what do you say, Burke?" Stallone said.

He didn't know if he was crazy. It was certainly possible at that point. But the sides of his mouth slowly curled into a smile. "I'm in."

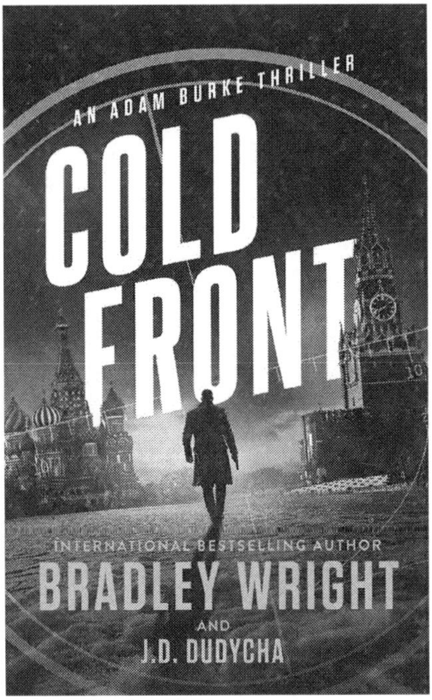

COLD FRONT
by
Bradley Wright and J.D. Dudycha
Book four in the
Adam Burke series will be
available in January!

ACKNOWLEDGMENTS

First and foremost, we want to thank you, the reader. We love what we do, and no matter how many people help us along the way, none of it would be possible if you weren't turning the pages.

To our family and friends. Thank you for always being there with mountains of support. You all make it easy to dream, and those dreams are what make it into these books. Without you, no fun would be had, much less novels be written.

To Deb Hall. Thank you for always taking our words and making them sound better. We are grateful for your edits, and your friendship.

To our advanced reader team. You continue to help make everything we do better. You all have become friends, and we thank you for catching those last few sneaky typos, and always letting us know when something isn't good enough. Adam Burke appreciates you, and so do Jon and I.

About the Author

Bradley Wright is the international bestselling author of espionage and mystery thrillers. BREAKING POINT is his twenty-sixth novel. Bradley lives with his family in Lexington, Kentucky. He has always been a fan of great stories, whether it be a song, a movie, a novel, or a binge-worthy television series. Bradley loves interacting with readers on Facebook, Twitter, and via email.

Join the online family:
www.bradleywrightauthor.com
info@bradleywrightauthor.com

ABOUT THE AUTHOR

J.D. Dudycha believes the best stories are written with characters overcoming real life struggles and everyone deserves a shot a redemption.

After a long stay in the baseball world, both as a player and a coach, J.D. has turned to his real passion, creating gritty, in-your-face characters who leap off the page and ooze practicality.

J.D. spends his time with his wife and children in Ponte Vedra, Florida. When he is able to step away from the world of writing fiction, he enjoys golf and fishing.

For more information visit:

Instagram: @JDDudycha